Struggle and Strife

Nick Gerrard

First Edition- Paperback
Published by
Breaking Rules Publishing Europe, 2021.
This is a work of fiction. Similarities to real people, places, or events are entirely coincidental.
Struggle & Strife
978-91-986840-4-9

Thanks to my lovely editor

Helen Baggott

Struggle & Strife art by www.marcelherms.nl

All of stories here were published first in the following literary publications, magazines, online and paperback anthologies.Breaking rules short story project, Litterati, Pikers press, The Ramingos Porch,The Rye Whiskey Review, Spillwords.com, Jotters United, The Siren magazine and Potato soup journal.

Content

The Powder Puffs Journey

-I can't stand English tea! Because when the Nazis left, we had nothing to eat or drink for two weeks or so. When the English arrived the first thing they gave us was tea, and we were all sick and since I cannot drink tea.

I raised my eyebrows and grinned at her. In my mind I pictured the Brits, faced with the horror, running round panicking this time.

-Jesus Christ, what the hell should we do?

-I don't know, mate, put the kettle on, and then we'll sort it all out.

I shrugged.

-Well, erm...

I giggled a little.

-Coffee then?

What Aunty Ruth was talking about was being in the camps. Liberated by the British, who forty-odd years later finds herself being breakfasted by another Brit from darkest

Birmingham, in an old Sudeten-Deutsche Lodge in the mountains on the border of Poland and the Czech Republic.

It had taken me a while to persuade Aunty Ruth to come visit us. She was never one to rough it. Ruth wanted the finer things in life, a little luxury, and who could blame her?

When I had first visited her at her artist husband's flat, we had partaken of coffee in the drawing room surrounded by art.

Cakes were served on blue patterned china, I grabbed at a coconut flecked jam sponge. The conversation stopped and all eyes turned.

I stopped and held the cake at my open gob.

My eyes moved left and right.

-What, what?

-We do have cake forks you know!

Of course, she did.

So, anyway, it had taken me ages to convince her that our little hideaway was of the highest standard, and it was.

Antique and rustic furniture mingled with communist relics and First Republic gadgets.

We picked her up from the train station and drove slowly through the blinding snowstorm. The smell and glow of oak welcomed her in.

She handed over two small packages. Two decorated paper bags. Inside two treasures were unwrapped.

-If you don't like them you can sell them.

We looked inside; I had a silver cigarette case, her husband's. My wife had a miniature powder-puff case, silver.

-No, no, we love them, thank you.

***

Ruth's husband's art was all over our place, this made her happy, and she looked at the picture of the farmhouse in Crete where they had managed to get to one year and smiled a little.

He had given some of it to us for a wedding present, this was when he was alive, well barely, as he was quite ill, and used a bag and a cane, as they had operated on the wrong leg.

I had admired the man and his art, so was very happy to receive the case. Unfortunate, then, that I had switched to electronic cigarettes six months before. But still, it looked nice on the bookcase.

The powder-puff case was another story.

Ruth's Great Uncle Oldrich had been in the Great War; reluctantly fighting for the Empire, against the British.

He was captured by the British and sent to a camp in Scotland. The prisoners were treated well, they never tried to escape, why would they? However, the weather did not agree with a lot of the middle-Europeans, and Ruth's Great Uncle became very ill with pneumonia.

-He was cared for very well, he said. The doctors were very kind. He had a fondness for your British tea too, which is funny.

The uncle returned to Moravia where he spent months and months in a special spa. He bathed in and drank smelly cloudy sulphur waters to help. Ruth visited as often as she could, she sang songs and read books to him, for comfort.

Now, during all this time he had done the lottery. Every week without fail he would place a little money on his lucky numbers. Even when he was away his wife had firm instructions to place money on the numbers.

Eventually his illness worsened, and they had to amputate his legs. The following week, he won the lottery.

He won!

He won a motorbike.

When he was well enough, he was told this by his wife, he laughed. He laughed for such a long time he brought on a coughing fit and was very ill again for a few days after. Eventually he got better and instructed his wife to sell the damn motorbike. When well enough to return home, his wife pushed his wheelchair around the plush department store in Brno as he picked out little presents for the people he loved. One of those presents was for his favourite little niece, and for her he picked out a very small powder-puff case. Just the right size for a little lady.

***

We were separated at school.

Suddenly the teachers got nasty.

Urging the other kids, our friends, to mock us.

Why? I didn't understand it.

'Why, Mama? What did we do wrong?'

There were few answers.

Some people came to our house. They seemed like police, but new police.

They took away my things. And all the bright things in the house. Anything pretty.

I hid the little powder-puff case in my special hiding place.

Uncle Oldrich had told me to take special care of it.

The nastiness and stupid things continued.

I couldn't understand it.

Nobody seemed to understand it.

We were made to sew the Star of David on our clothes.

Our neighbour's shops were burnt or left windowless after a night of rain and a morning of sun that left the streets sparkling and smoking.

An old lady spat in my father's face as he held my hand on the way home from school for the last time.

I held his hand so tight.

If I held his hand, I thought everything would be alright.

'Why can't I go to school, Dada?'

'Don't worry, Ruth, one day you will go back.'

'But, Dada, I am a good student, why can't I go to school, I don't understand?'

'Some people don't want us there, Ruth, bad people... but they won't always be there. We have seen this before. Things will go back to normal; you will see.'

'Do you promise?'

'I promise.'

I could see in his eyes that he hadn't really promised. Not like when he promised to take me to the boating lake, or to buy me the flowery dress in Mr Benes's window.

It wasn't a promise like the one when he told me about the huge slices of cake and ice cream, he would buy me for my birthday in the Tivoli Kavarna.

Now, his eyes showed fear and I knew he couldn't keep his promise.

Mr Polosky's shop was all burned out, and I didn't know where he had gone. Many people, our neighbours, had just gone. One minute they were there, then they disappeared.

My best friend, Eva, was gone, she didn't even say goodbye.

No one would say where people had gone.

My mother came home and sat at the table. She burst into tears, her head in her hands.

My father stood over her, stroking her long black hair.

She had been sent home from the hospital, where she helped the new babies.

Others in our street and around were sent home. People stopped working.

We had to queue for food, awful food.

My father was still able to help his patients. But was given no medicine to help them.

He pleaded at the community centre to the more important men in our community. They did nothing to help him.

The queues got longer.

The new uniformed people started to order us around, not just the new police force, but people who had been our friends, our neighbours. They began to shout at us.

Some came and argued with my father in the street, by the lines of people waiting to see him.

They pushed people away, and sometimes hit them. And screamed in their faces.

I wanted it all to end. At night I closed my eyes and tried to wish it all away.

It felt like when I had a bad dream and I couldn't reach something or couldn't run fast enough, and tried to wake myself up, because I knew I was dreaming, but couldn't wake up.

It felt like this.

***

The street shook from heavy trucks. I looked out of the window. They were all over the square.

Orders were being shouted out in a nasty sounding German. Red-cheeked men in helmets clattered out of the trucks, busy as ants. They all looked very disorganised, until they were ordered to halt. And then like mechanical ants they were all in order.

The soldiers entered all the buildings, shouting and shouting, pushing and pushing, making people leave their apartments. Doors were booted in. Office workers were hurried into the street. People grabbed coats and boots.

We went down quickly; we didn't want the ants to come inside our home. We were pushed by guns under the baroque arches of the square. Those of us who had coats and the shirtless office workers.

The mayor of the town, Mr Sheller, was busy, his red face was redder than usual, and his usual lovingly greased moustache was a bit shabby! He hurried and complained about being pushed. And he straightened his top hat and pushed his bursting waistcoat out. And wanted to know what the meaning of this was.

I remember these words.

'What is the meaning of this, I am no Jew, why are we being pushed around?'

The other office workers mumbled complaints also, mainly to the new police, as the soldiers stood a little way off, not talking, or moving, just watching. The police ordered silence.

We were separated, girls with mothers.

I cried as they dragged, shoved and beat men and boys onto waiting lorries. People screamed, people begged, people pleaded.

I held out my arms desperately, trying to reach someone.

I ran after the trucks as they left.

That was the last time I saw my dada and my brothers.

I knew we were going to be taken away, so I managed to run into our flat and take the powder-puff case from under the floorboards. I hid it in my knickers thinking that no one would look there.

***

-So, what happened?

-Well, my mother and I were taken by train to Terrazin camp, you know of this yes?

-Sure.

-The journey was terrible. One bucket for a toilet and one of a foul-smelling water. We slept all bodies entwined, out of necessity and for the need of warmth.

Things were not so bad there; I mean not so bad as what I experienced later.

We were overcrowded, but there was some food and some normal life. I even went to school, not a normal school, just some classes given by teachers.

But many people died. I was afraid and cried all the time, my mother covered my eyes, but couldn't stop me seeing.

I became a woman. My childhood taken from me.

There were tradesmen, carpenters and toolmakers, cobblers and tailors. My mother found a cobbler who put a special heel on my boot, somewhere I could hide the case.

In the dormitories we slept two, three to a bunk with one sheet.

After some weeks we were put onto train waggons again. We travelled for weeks.

When we arrived at the station on our final stop, we were told that this was an educational work camp.

Some thousand or so people were separated and as we stood shivering. We heard volley after volley of shots in the distance.

We were a few hundred left now, all women. Other women were marched to other such camps.

Our huts were basic, with a stove. We had little fuel, but we scraped enough together to have some heat. We were allowed to mingle freely in the parade ground.

We listened to stories and rumours of all sorts, hope, no hope, savagery, kindness, slaughter, rehabilitation. Rescue.

We were made to work in the forests and the quarry. The work was exhausting. We were given soup and black bread.

Our guards were Estonians or Russians. Some were kind, some not. Some gave us extra food and smiles.

My mother was taken ill with typhoid as were many, they were not cared for but taken away, I don't know where.

One guard was taken by my friend Tasha, who had comforted me after my mother left. We snuggled in my bunk and tried to give some of the love back that had been taken away from our lives; we slept, in embrace, holding a comfort.

This guard Otto smiled at first, tipped his hat, then talked more and more to Tasha when he could, and gave her chocolate. Chocolate! It was as if a fairy prince has given her a palace of gold. We shared the chocolate, at night, under blankets.

Otto and Tasha took great risks in trying to meet and just talk.

One day Otto gave Tasha a small red lipstick... There were no mirrors in the camp.

What does someone need with a lipstick in hell?

None of us had even looked at ourselves for a long time, only in the reflection of water.

At night, when no one was looking, I unlocked my shoe hiding place and gave her the powder-puff case. She cried when she looked at herself, blotched red face, matted hair, scratches, scars, and oldness.

We girls scrubbed her face and body, and with much pain tried to untangle her hair.

The day was a holiday for the guards, and a day of rest for us. The atmosphere was relaxed. We snuck away and got out the case again. And with no one watching she applied the red lipstick and then walked to the fence, to Otto.

He looked at her for a short time... we were huddled together watching from a short distance.

He looked at her and tears rolled down his cheeks. He didn't speak, he took off his hat and with a sweep of his hand before him he bowed. Towards a woman.

***

-Jesus, what a story!

-And what happened?

-Otto and Sophie planned an escape... under cover of darkness. We all collected little food and clothes, the best as we could manage. She left dressed as an Estonian day worker. And we heard nothing for days. Then we heard rumours; they had escaped to Scandinavia; they had been shot.

We all clung to the story of our Romeo and Juliet. That was our hope, our fantasies under the rough blankets at night.

We heard nothing for a few weeks, and we had hope.

But one day we all stopped work and walked to the wire and watched in shock and disappointment as they were marched back through the camp.

They untied their hands and made them stand straight in front of a firing squad against a fence with the expanse of the wilderness behind them. As they tried to reach for each other's hands a volley of shots ripped into their bodies. As the echoes faded the brownness of their bodies let out a glow of steam as the red stained the white of the snow and seeped into the mud, their fingers were touching.

***

-And your mother?

-I never knew what happened to her at the time.

We were moved on very quickly, into wagons again, there were no sick or old this time. We travelled for days, to the final camps.

-Oh my god, so sorry.

-Don't be sorry, it was not your fault...

-Yes but...

-There is nothing one can say of these things... I cried for sure, but I had to live... to live for us both.

But one thing I must tell you about the powder puff. Before we left another friendly guard called Libor warned us not to take anything we had hidden, these camps would be in Germany and Poland and much worse. I sat all night thinking if to trust this man. I did... I gave him my powder-puff case and he promised to hide it for me, and maybe one day if I could, I would go and he would return it to me.

-And you went back?

-You are a very impatient man... We were taken to the extermination camps. And I was one of the few who survived. I was lucky.

You have read all about these camps I take it, so I won't bore you with the details.

-Bore me...

After the liberation, after months of being logged in and out, made well, documented, pushed here, taken there, injected here... I eventually made it back to Brno. I was placed in a care home, and they cared for me.

-And what about the case?

-There's another chapter to come, let's have more coffee and I'll tell it.

***

In the 1960s I applied to visit Estonia to visit the camp where my mother died. The red tape was terrible; the authorities didn't want the past raked up, so made it terribly difficult for me to get a travel permit.

I wrote to a professor of art in Estonia who knew of my husband and who had fought against the Nazis.

We corresponded and he pulled strings, wrote letters, called in favours; did everything he could to get me a travel pass. When it arrived, or I should say they arrived, as there were mountains of documents, I cried.

The journey was long, I took it alone and at every official juncture my journey was hindered. I passed through scenery I seemed to remember, this time in a fairly comfortable little carriage. The people were very polite to me except the border guards, and at every frontier I was taken in for questioning, and to have all my papers checked over and over again.

I eventually made it to Tallinn and met the professor, who gave me shelter in his apartment, and made me most welcome. We journeyed to the place where the camp used to be. This was the saddest part for me, the most vivid memories came back into my mind. We visited the village close by. We were met by the mayor, a courteous man, but again I was questioned by local party members, and had my papers checked and checked. We were taken to a small graveyard near to the outside of the old camp that was now a pig farm. There was a little graveyard, with flowers, and little wooden crosses... there was a plaque commemorating the women who had died there, and there was my mother's name. I knew she must have died, but one always lives with a faint hope if one has not been told the full truth. This was my mother's resting place. I thanked them all. They were happy to receive a relative of one of the people from the camps. Happy to know that I, a person, had survived, and was here to visit. They were happy for someone to see that they cared that they remembered. I was left alone looking at the commemoration plaque. A youngish woman approached me. She told me her father had been at the camp and that he had promised to keep something for one of the girls. She felt I should have it. She unwrapped a red lace handkerchief, and inside was the powder-puff case.

***

-No way! Sounds too unbelievable to be true! And you brought it all the way back here... wow.

-These little stories are not so unbelievable, not compared to the unbelievable things that went on. These things, these little stories, coincidences, these little fates are our hope, our reality, our faith if you wish.

It was by no means easy. I had to hide it in my knickers again. The communist authorities were always suspicious of anything connected with the war, and often stole things or hid things away, but what half-drunk half-witted jobsworth would search the knickers of an old woman like me?

She giggled.

- So, I took many train journeys once again with the case hidden. But this time the journey was home.

But you must understand that at that time people were reluctant to speak about the war, the past.

After the revolution in Czechoslovakia my husband, who was a great traveller, went back with me to visit my mother's resting place and we put an urn with her name on it. Quite a few villagers came and stood with hats in their hands.

And I stood with them, with the powder-puff grasped tightly in my hand.

Behind the Orange Bike and Grill

Outside the triumphal arch stands the orange bike and grill. Behind it stand I, Waffle Paul. I am also dressed in orange, with a shiny pink head. Steam is coming out of the iron and from the top of my head. An aroma of toast and toffee wafts over and hits the noses of wrapped-up Berliners and stops their rushing, just for a moment.

-My dear, come on over, let my sweet delights warm your cold nose today.

The little girl grins back and inches her way over; head down, body bobbing, eyes glimpsing up.

-This recipe comes from my granma back in old Amsterdam, the recipe is a secret, so shhh...! I share it only with you!

-You, sir, with your wonderful Russian hat, come on, take a bite!

-Madam, your beauty is clear for all to see. Look at the roses blooming from your cheeks!

I take a hot waffle from the iron, cut it carefully then dip my favourite knife into the syrup and spread it; I wrap it in a little paper envelope, smile, bow my head and wave my arm in front of me.

-You're welcome.

That day I see a shape lying on a bench. I glance at it, moving, in-between servings and banter. The young woman yawns and stretches and gathers her blanket around her with her fingertip-holed gloves. I catch her gaze, I try a little grin of comfort; she smiles back, briefly.

In the winter months, I would pop along to the Gates on a Wednesday afternoon, just to cheer people up in the mid-week gloom. In summer I am around for a couple of days, I like to think I am a part of people's lives; a drop off from a walk home, a stop off for young lovers; a treat for grandads to give to wild-ginger-haired granddaughters.

But In winter I come out of love, ha ha! Of course, I do it to make money, but, you know, I make more from the cultural conventions, and Christmas markets, and these days I am happy I can choose what work I do, sometimes for money sometimes for other reasons.

On other days, I guide old-Dutch visitors around abandoned beauties. I sing songs on barges and whisper interesting facts in museums. I take survivors and school parties past memorials and through now thriving bohemian ghettos.

-And as you walk around you will notice the Stolpersteins, these gold tiles commemorate victims of the Nazis; please wipe your feet on them. Don't worry! Before the war, it was the custom for Germans who tripped over a protruding cobblestone to remark-

'There must be a Jew buried here.' They are placed here for you to trip over, to draw your attention to people who once lived or worked here but were taken from here. I hold my orange umbrella in the air.

-Ladies and gentlemen, onwards! Please stumble over and remember!

I work late into the afternoon, a figure walks slowly across the grass, a floppy hat and bulging layers of clothes. She carries her backpack to the bench, takes out a book and reads. When we are the only two around, I do a little fox-trot behind the grill...

-My dear, may I offer you a sizzlingly syrupy waffle?

-I'm sorry, are you talking to me?

-Yes, I am. Come here, come! Please take one.

-I'm sorry, I have no money.

-No, no; no money, it's for free.

-I'm sorry I cannot take it.

-I see you are a proud person, this is not charity, Waffle Paul gives no charity. I give only gifts, to beautiful people.

-I am not beautiful.

-You, my dear, are a like a blooming foxglove, with eyes of toasted almonds and skin to match my waffle syrup.

A smile appears, she walks over, and I perform.

-Madame.

-Thank you.

She nibbles and breathes in trying to cool it down.

-It's... Oh... hot! – Delicious though. Thank you again.

-It's my pleasure. Do you mind?

-No, please.

I join her on the bench and light a small cigar.

-Where are you from?

– I'm Turkman, from Iraq.

-Turkestan?

-No, everyone says that, no, I'm from Iraq, but I am a Turkman.

-Sorry, I didn't quite catch it. Do you want some soup? I have some fresh pumpkin and coconut. I love my soups! I pour a beaker full from the flask and hand the lid to her.

-There you go.

She cups her two hands and blows.

-I'm sorry, I haven't asked you your name, my name is Paul.

-Akgul.

-Akgul. That's a lovely name, does it mean anything?

-White flower.

-Aha! Yes, I guessed right.

I send a smoke ring into the sky.

A couple of giggling office girls stroll up to the cart.

-I'll be back in a jiffy.

-Beautiful ladies, how you bring joy to my life, let me bring joy to yours.

When I come back, she is walking away; she looks back, hands in her coat, and smiles. I look out for her the next few days, but she doesn't appear.

Then on the following Thursday, I spot her strolling. Akgul approaches; sits down and takes a plastic box out of a bag. I walk over.

-Hi, long time no see, I thought you had disappeared.

-No, just busy, nice to see you again, do you have time for a little lunch now?

-You brought lunch, perfect! I was just thinking of packing up for a bit, it's quiet now after the rush.

-Good, It's not much I'm afraid.

-Not much, this is great.

I rub my hands and sit. She delves into the bag.

-I have Iranian e kalbas sandwiches and pistachio cake.

I take a bite.

-Mm, delicious.

-You should try this, it's Doogh; it's a typical minty yogurt drink from back home.

We sit and eat quietly for a while.

-May I ask you something.

-Of course, go ahead.

-I'm sorry, this is delicious by the way, you have brought this lovely food and here am I thinking you were maybe homeless. She laughs a little.

-You're right, I was. But I have a place in a hostel now. And we have a shared kitchen, and nearby are lots of Arab and Turkish shops, so I was able to get the ingredients, and I baked the cake myself.

We smile at each other, and then both look out into the distance and chew away.

-Sorry, I don't mean to be nosey, but how long were you homeless for?

-It's fine, only for a short time but it was not the best of times. I was scared, and cold and hungry, and slept in doorways and parks, wherever I could, wherever was quiet and dry, but I had to leave, I had to make the move.

I look at her and wait to see if she wants to add more.

-You are wondering what I left, how I came to be here?

-It's fine, you don't have to talk; it's fine.

-No, it's OK, I don't mind, it's good to talk, I think.

I try to smile; try to reassure her a little.

-It was the war, right?

-The war, there's always war. Never good. Fighting on all sides. Murders between peoples. Our people were never treated fairly in Iraq, and now, well, many died. It was the worst of times.

-But you got out, you escaped?

-Women and girls were taken, some just disappeared. Many women were kidnapped for husbands even before the war. My father decided to try to protect me from various armies and IS. At that time there were lots of men coming to try to arrange weddings, offering money to families in exchange for daughters. Although my family needed money, I think my father didn't give me away for the money. His idea was to protect me. He could see no other way to protect me. He wanted me to go to the West, to safety, but also, I think he wanted me to have a chance in life, and he thought that sending me to the West, was the best option. What chance is there now over there?

-Must have been awful for you but I can understand your father wanting the best for you, but it must have been terrible thing for him to do too.

-Maybe. I know he wanted a good life for me, but I cannot forgive him for what he did. His own daughter! I can't understand how he could do it.

-I cannot begin to understand how you must feel and also how he must have felt.

I look at her. I wipe my mouth and hands on the paper napkin and empty the rubbish in the bin.

-Thank you for the wonderful meal, and I always like to enjoy a little cigar after a meal, would you like one?

-Yes, I have taken to smoking a little since I arrived here, but only cigarettes, but a cigar would be lovely, my papa smoked cigars.

We sit and drag and smile at each other a little.

She came by once a week after that. We shared lunch, both contributing. Salads of pulses and fresh herbs from her, turmeric butternut soups from my flask. And we always finished with a little coffee and hot waffles; a story, a smile and a little laughter, a tear or two, and a vanilla cigar.

***

We move from the bench to cafes and bistros; I show her some of favourite haunts.

-What'll you have? I'm having a cappuccino and apple pie.

-I'll have hot chocolate and chocolate fudge cake. It's lovely here, I love the old paintings, and the old ladies are very charming.

-Yes, this is one of my favourite cafes, one of the oldest in Berlin, traditional Jewish, well it was, the Jewish school is just over the road.

-And your family lived around here?

-No, not at all, I just so happened to end up here in this area after the wall came down. I always lived near it, but after lots of young people moved into this area because it was cheap.

-It seems quite fashionable now.

-It's getting that way yes, more and more hipsters. It used to be quite alternative, quite arty. The edge has gone a bit now, but I still love it, maybe it has mellowed like me.

-Have you mellowed?

-I think I've mellowed yes, through age, and necessity.

-Necessity?

-Well, let's just say I lived a pretty wild life and now I have to take care of myself a little more.

-A wildlife? You! Really? What kind of things did you get up to? If I'm not being too nosy.

-Not at all. Well, I was a bit of a hippy for a while. So, lots of squatting, lots of drinking, and parties, also a lot of political protests. There were happenings and drugs a plenty too. Yeah, well, too much really and for many years, drinking into the small hours. My health was affected quite a lot.

-Really!

-But, you're OK now?

-I still drink but not like I used to. And I don't go out as much anymore either, and try and be a bit healthier, I had some problems with my liver a few years ago but I am a bit better now. I looked at her, we had something now; I needed to get it all out.

-I have to confess a little here, I did spend a short time in prison.

-Prison! You're kidding, what for?

-No, I was on a demo and the cops just started laying into this friend of mine, a little guy, and basically, I steamed in, and well, I hurt one cop pretty badly.

-How long did you spend there?

-I got six months.

-Was it bad?

-Not too bad, I got stick from the guards but the guys were OK with me. And I started a degree in politics and history inside.

-Really, I wondered where you went to university, now I know.

She giggled behind her hand.

-Yeah, Yeah, very funny. I finished a degree later, once I got back to the hippy life in the squats then I finished at a university, part-time. What about you? You seem quite well-educated.

-Why thank you, well my father was a big community man and a small politician; and encouraged me to study. I loved history and my interest in politics was passed from my father. I loved to study actually, but it was difficult. I also ran a small gift shop, little artefacts of Turkman memorabilia. I sold these to Iraqi and foreign visitors. It wasn't much but it helped my family.

-So, you didn't finish your studies?

-I'm afraid not. Because of cultural reasons my father was prevented from working in the big offices, he could only work with the local community, for presents. I had to leave university because of lack of money. My mother washed other families' clothes, and my store's small takings contributed, and with the presents from the community for my father's intelligent advice and decision making we managed to live. My life before the troubles was wonderful, I had no problems growing up, it was only later. I still love my home, and although I hate him for what he did, I still love my papa.

I lean over and wipe some cream from her corner lip. She looks in my eyes and just for a moment, a little moment holds my hand close to her mouth, squeezes, and I feel a tug right in my solar plexus, from here to here.

The Ballhouse.

After the wall came down someone found a key and opened up a derelict to discover a peeling elegance that had been hidden away. The chance to prance and dream and whirl your love around chained up. The place has been spruced up but not changed, fixed up but not modified; dusted down but the memories left. In the garden sat hipster families, would-be artists, students and elegant old Jewish ladies; gossiping over large carrot cakes with proper silver forks, stirring cinnamon topped coffees in long glasses, seated at miss-matching metal tables, amongst the cracked slabs and flower pots. All sat enjoying a new-found bohemian chic, built on the ruins of a restrictive stupidity. All waiting for a night. Waiting for a booking to be confirmed, waiting for a table to dance.

As you walk in a gentleman in a bow tie and greased back grey hair takes your coat at the cloakroom. A tuxedoed hipster in a top hat, docs and dreadlocks checks the tickets and holds open the door and bows, whilst keeping eager ticketless punters at bay.

The main dining hall fills up; motorbike jackets and fur coats are carried by waiters. From the stage, the gay instructor sets the music and jumps down to the wooden floor.

A young man with no rhythm and a lover who is desperate for a partner, tries to keep up with his hopeful steps. The instructor steps in; shows him how it's done. After half an hour the crowd applauds him back to his seat, his lover smiling widely, holding his hand tightly.

Kids are set down, tables are filled, and smokers cluster in the garden.

Waiters dart in and out of dancers and kids skidding, and jagged-edged tables, jutting out chairs. Then the dancing starts for real. First, come the professionals, the sixty-plus guys, well versed in the moves. The men in ill-fitting moth smelling red jackets and faded patterned ties. The ladies, for they are ladies, in thrown together remnants of balls long gone. They glide over the floor, empty for them only, not a rule, just out of respect. Latin rhythms dance around the high ceilings, as the couples live for a moment in the spotlights.

Steaks on slates mixed with Wagner, pizzas on planks rolled with a Bolero. A German eighties dance tune, another carafe of red, laughter, chat and a Beatles medley. An old beery singalong; the dance floor fills with full people, the disco ball twists a little lighter, the strobe lights flicker faster. Eighty-year-olds groove to Abba, teenagers jive to Bowie. Partners are swapped and everyone, everyone, lets it all hang out.

Me and Akgul enter, dressed up in our best black, the doormen take our overcoats. The band is warming up. We are shown to a table. We order wine, clink glasses. My friends arrive.

My tall scruffy friend shakes her hand.

-And you must be the lovely lady we have heard so much about. Adam, charmed.

– I am so very glad to meet you all, I've heard so much about you all I feel like I know you already.

-And this is Evette.

My favourite bottle blonde is dressed in charming hippy chic.

-My dear, I'm so happy to meet you.

-Thank you, me too, very much!

-So, guys, let me order some wine, and then we can get some food.

Tumblers of scarlet wine are filled, and again. Plates of cheese and dried strawberries on large off-white plates, smeared with quaffed quince jelly are laid down for starters.

Steaming meatballs held in the air are weaved through an assault course; wafting liver and thyme mixing with Black Velvet scent over the backs of strapless dresses.

-So, you were saying...

I smiled, Evette was stroking her arm, I knew she would get her to open up.

-The men paid my father and they arranged for me to come to Germany to wed a Turkish man.

The journey was terrible, we were in cramped trucks, bumping and banging all night. There was crying and cold, driving for days, with little water or food. The smell was what I remember the most, there was only a bucket in a corner with a held sheet for privacy, and no one washed. Yes, the smell was the worst thing. The smell was of fear, always the smell, always the fear.

We guys go smoke outside; on the way we greet friends working there, and laugh and slap backs of old drinking partners, and I pretend-punch in the belly an old comrade from the battles with police.

I look through the steamed-up window; I can see the two women talking, arms linked, heads together.

-So, tell me about the marriage, now that we are friends, and no holds barred!

-So, I met my future husband eventually, he was a very boring man, not interested in me at all, he took me back to his family home. He needed me because his first wife had died. I was given a small room, every day was cleaning, washing, cooking, ironing. There were a lot of family members in this house, and many rooms, and a lot of mess to clean. The women were never satisfied. My husband just sat there, eating; wiping juice on his sleeve as he pushed me out of the way of the television.

-Gosh, I don't know what to say to that. I'm sorry.

-I'm sorry, Evette, I have made you uncomfortable. You have had enough of my story.

-No, please, it's just I really don't know what to say to you, I'm sorry doesn't seem enough somehow, but please carry on.

-Sorry, yes, eventually we got married, just a small family event really, my husband was not interested; he just did what the women said. On our wedding night, he went to sleep.

-You should think yourself lucky by the sounds of it.

-Yes, you are right. And thankfully he only made me do it a couple of times. Eventually, I became pregnant. I was still made to clean the house and work though. When my little Adalet was born I took care of him, but the other women looked after him more and more and I was treated less well than before.

Evette smiles and rubs the top of her hand on the table

– I was happy to be legal but not happy to be stuck with a man who didn't know me, didn't want me, and I worried for my son, the family kept me apart from him more and more.

-And to marry without love is a tragedy, no.

-Yes, I believe that.

I glimpse through the window again, just checking, I see the two women look at each other, smirk, then start laughing. I grin.

***

We walk through the street stalls in the old market building selling tastes from the world. I order six oysters with oxtail vinaigrette and grated horseradish, take two glasses of sparkling wine, and some mini Spanish tapas and we bunch up on a bench.

-Don't chew; just let it slither down your throat. Good?

-I'm not sure, it's a bit weird.

-Try the serrano.

She slips a slice in and we both sip the wine.

-Now I feel good. So, how come you sell waffles?

-Whoosh! Right out of the blue!

I love that about her. I love her freeness with questions and opinions, no holding back for fear of social constraints. I giggle and take up a storyteller's pose.

-Now let me see, I have done many things in my life. I was a teacher, a leftie activist as you know, back in the seventies, I also sang in bands and...

-You sang in bands? You never mentioned that!

-Yeah, singing in bands, selling waffles... tours, all showbiz!

I roll my flat cap down from my balding head into my hand and bow.

-I had some wild times but I am older now, so not much singing I'm afraid, I have to live a quieter life. Actually, I am happy to live a little quieter life now. I was always interested in politics and history, what with my Dutch, Jewish, Hungarian roots. In the old days I was on the barricades, but as you get older, you know. The Stolpersteins became very important to me; I helped set them up as you know.

-And the waffles?

-Yeah sorry, the waffles. The waffles came about because I loved doing the tours but was fed up of having no money. I love selling the waffles, I love the contact with people; it feels like an extension of the tours, to be honest. An extension of me too.

-Thank you.

-For what?

-For talking to me.

-I'm happy you feel that way; that is what good friends are for.

-And are we good friends now?

-I sure hope so.

-Me too.

Akgul places her hand over my knee.

***

I walk with Akgul through a little alley at the side of a kebab bar, I go and sit at the bar, a man manipulates mashed lamb round a metal rod and places it next to others and skewers of red marinated slashed pieces of meat; a grill of charcoal sends out bursts of steam and crackles. A man next to me washes his saliva away with a small cold glass of beer and a puff of a Murad; we nod to each other and I do the same. The women's centre next door is just a few rooms, with a kitchen and a central relaxing room full of kids and leaflets and settees and chatter. Women are flipping breads on griddles, thick white arms tossing leaves, thick fingers folding thin pastry; delicate hennaed hands crush corns, shell nuts. And laughter and smiles, and big voices booming instructions, advice. She leaves me in the kebab house and goes in.

Akgul told me she sits in a circle with women on couches, women knitting on chairs, some flopping out breasts without breaking their chat. Dazzling scarfs cover deep cream eyes, some braid long silky hair others brush.

-It's not so easy to leave. It took me two a and a half years after Adalet was born.

-We understand, it is never easy.

-I got beaten very badly when I was seen talking to other Iranian women, in a coffee house.

-Some guys are like that, some guys are living in the last century still; you know that from home, no?

-Yes, there are men like that, there are communities like that, IS wanted us all to be like that.

-We are lucky here, we have a mixture of secular and more liberal people, the real fanatics have not much power here; you are free here to speak, so please go ahead.

-We all have our problems, well most of us, but we all have problems with our men, that's why we are here, you will even see non-Muslim women come here, problems are not only for us

-I decided I couldn't carry on, and even if it meant me not seeing my son it was better to leave and try to be happy and try to get him out somehow. I waited for my chance, and packed some of my things, and left. I spent a few months sleeping where I could.

I met the Iranian women, at the stores again. We went for coffee when I could, they were very angry about my situation; they took me to a centre, where I spoke to workers who got me into the hostel.

-And what about your son, and the family?

-The family are always looking for me. My son, I have no chance to see him now.

***

We grow much closer still. What were little flirtatious strokes and touches become cuddles and passionate embraces. During a boat ride down the Spree and passing under the Weidendammer bridge, and staring up at the lovers' locks, we kissed, for the first time. Then we walked hand in hand with a basket and blanket up to the Teufelsberg tower on the hill and ate our lunch, and I lean over and kiss her again, softly but passionately.

And love tastes of coconut and coriander; vanilla smoke and waffle syrup.

***

In a social centre, a bare room with a few help posters, a blue Formica table, three metal chairs. A bland social worker is taking notes. I stand outside in a corridor of windows, walking up and down; I can just see their heads through the glass.

-But I'm not really a refugee.

-But you were sent away to escape the war?

-But I was married, I was sent by my family to have a better life, I was a bride.

-Yes, but we are interested in why you left.

-That's easy; my father wanted a better life for me, but life was better back there, here was hell.

-But you escaped a war... and

-Look, there are many immigrants like me, not refugees, just immigrants, who are here for other reasons than escaping war, our story is never told. Yes, there was a war; there is always war, but...

-So, basically, you were trafficked?

-My god, not really, no, not sold into the sex trade, but I was sent by my family, but what I was sent to is like slavery, so yes, like a sex slave, not like you mean but I felt like a whore.

-But you were not a prostitute? And you came here illegally?

-Are you listening to me? Yes, I was illegal at first but then I became legal, but I was used as a slave, and as for sex work, I think being forced to marry a man, and then having my child taken away is being used as a sex worker. There are many women here who have the same experience, and god knows how many who cannot come to this place that are stuck in this situation. You should help them; you should help me. I want my baby back.

-But your husband says you left, you are not a good mother; do you have any proof, any witnesses?

-You have my word.

-It's not enough.

-There are many women here in the same situation, you must help us.

-We do help them; we will do what we can.

-It's not enough.

#

I am doing a boat tour; I am my usual self; bouncing up and down, talking double Dutch into the mike. Akgul is smiling, the people are laughing, she cannot understand the language but knows I am quite funny. I finish to applause and titters, and take a whiskey and sit at the back next to her. She kisses me on the check. After drifting on my shoulder as the boat passes Museum Island, she straightens up and sips her juice and...

-I want my son back, Paul.

-And we can get him back, the courts will find in your favour.

-I think they won't, they will say I am not a fit mother; they have lots of witnesses ready to lie.

-But we have witnesses too, we can...

-They will win.

I squeeze her shoulder. She flicks my hand away and faces the window.

-Those bloody bastards will keep my son... they are terrible people, I don't want my son there, I need him with me.

-So, what can we do?

-I don't know. I know though I can offer my son a good life now, and a better one than living there... I don't want him to be a part of that family, what kind of a man will he grow into? What kind of a life do they have planned for him? And I am his mother he needs me! And I need him! He is my son, Paul, he is me, and I want him back!

She starts to cry into his shoulder.

-We can win.

She stiffens.

-You are so sure, I am not. You, who hates authority so much, suddenly believes in the system. I talked to other mothers, and they say I have little chance.

-But what else is there, we have to try.

-I will take him. I will steal him back if I have to.

-Steal him?

-Take him, steal him, whatever, but steal him back from those people. Will you help me?

-Will I help you? Taking a child, I don't know, maybe we should just wait for the courts? I have a friend who is a lawyer, maybe we should ask him for advice and...

-I cannot wait, Paul. Wait for what? For more advice, more court dates, more social workers prying into my life, more lies, more fights. Help me, Paul. Please.

I turn my head.

She told me later what happened.

The women beat her, the husband beat her. But they were happy to get someone to wipe the kids' arses, someone to skivvy and cook, someone to bully.

On the lovers' lock bridge Akgul walks towards me; her face is bruised.

-Look at you! That's it, I'm gonna fucking kill this guy.

-No, Paul, don't do this please, we must wait, we must...

-Fuck this, no one should have to put up with this... the

-Paul, listen to me! We will wait and bide our time... please, we have to wait!

I stomp around huffing and puffing, with my hands on the back of my head.

-I should fucking kill this guy.

-We will in our own time, in our own way, we'll get him.

***

I park the car in the alley round the corner from the little launderette the night before. She packs her small bundle of things and hides them. The other women in the house are busy, baking cakes and sweets and doing each other's nails and hair, as usual.

The family arrives at the Ballhouse late, as was expected. My friend's fake free prize-tickets to the dance had been happily accepted of course. Who wouldn't pass up a free evening of wine and food? They are seated and drinks supplied. They order almost everything on the menu, and more drinks.

Akgul's husband eats with his mouth open, the grease from the meatballs dripping in his drool as he sits watching the twisting young girls on the floor. The children are wiped and smacked and a huge mess grows on the table. The hefty wooden doors to the elegant gallery are opened by two top-hatted, tattooed-neck, black-suited and booted doormen.

She completed her chores and shakily, breathlessly replaces some of the washing with her things, and covers them. She puts on their coats and Adalet in a kid carrier attached to her front, securely, and walks out, slowly.

Akgul enters on the tips of their hands. She slips the black shawl off her bare shoulders slightly and swans through the parting crowds on the edge of the floor, near to the cocktail bar. A waiter with a huge tray turns and glides the tray over her head. The pearl buttons on her tasselled purple top glisten in the disco lights, bouncing little lasers of light beams. Her long silk green skirt almost covers her suede brown ankle boots. Her husband and the table stop mid-gulp to stare, shocked and open gobbed. She passes him, and he makes a grab, but she shrugs him off and waiters appear in front of him, in front of his face.

-More wine, sir?

The maître de takes her shawl and helps her up onto a stool at the bar. The barman mixes a Cosmopolitan. She takes the glass, sips the pink liquid, turns and surveys the crowd.

-Why was he taking so long?

-One thirty he said, one thirty!

She looks out of the launderette window; just normal Berliners going about it all. I push my face up against the steamed-up window and grin widely.

First I was afraid I was petrified... the song rings out. People part and I stand; I stride to the far end of the floor; the other dancers move to the edges.

And I grew strong.... And I learned how to get along.

-Sorry, bloody traffic, I'm parked in the alley. Are you ready?

-Yes, I think it's safe.

-OK, you take the boy I'll go ahead with the stuff, put it in the car and be ready. You come five minutes after me.

-Alright.

I take a last look around out of the window and squeeze her hand.

-Let's go.

I see something. She sees my face change and speeds up.

-Akgul... No!

A hand comes from behind, grabs her shoulder and pulls her, she turns and a fist smacks into her face.

-Thought you could deceive me uh? You dirty fucking whore.

She drops to her knees, grasping her son to her breast. The hand goes up again. I am running, gaining speed.

-No!

I am getting closer.

The husband looks up. As I get faster and closer, I reach into my jacket and pull out my favourite knife. Before he can react, I thrust it into his chest. We both fall with the momentum.

The waiters stand guard over the family's table and around the floor, the crowd are pushing in too, no one has returned to their seats.

I stand, look at my hands, I have blood on them, I look at the guy and wipe my hands on his clean trousers. He tries to get up, clutching the knife, he falls back, he tries again but falls back.

The family look on, they see they have lost.

As the music fades, the doormen help us on with our coats. The waiters stand guard over the family's table and around the floor, the crowd still haven't returned to their seats. The husband moves, but my friends move quicker, grabbing his shoulders holding him back. Akgul hands Adalet to me, walks over and spits in her husband's face.

Just turn around now, and walk out the door.

I grab Akgul's arm.

-Let's go!

She turns to look, stuck. I push her towards the door.

-Let's go, forget about him! Come on move!

I stop, turn, look back at the man. The man is trying to get up but keeps fainting back, I look at him for about fifteen seconds, shake my head, then we turn around; and walk away.

***

We packed what we could and drove all night. Across unmanned borders, over Slavic and Austro lands, and finally to Budapest. To a flat of family members, a shared flat for those still left. A flat left by those who were taken and never came back. It was now a refuge for those in need. We stayed for a few weeks and discussed the situation with friends, good solid friends. Eventually, it was decided to go to the small Hungarian quarter of the large Serb town, where no one would look, where no one would tell.

We built a new waffle stand.

-My dear, come on over, let my sweet delights warm your cold nose today.

His smile is wide; the little boy wraps the warm delight uptight and hands it over with a smile.

-This recipe came from my aunty back in old Berlin, the recipe is a secret, so shhh!

I share it only with you.

Zazous and the Rats

The black windowless vans pulled up down the street. I slunk back into the doorway of the cafe, out of the rain and away from the terror. The raid wasn't here thankfully. The black squads entered an apartment block, storming up the stairs, batons drawn.

A leader in a blue suit is bored and starts strolling up the street towards me, looking around the place, checking. I made myself known, I stepped out and lit a Gitanne and shoved my face high.

-What is this place?

-Just a bar, just a place to drink, chat, read a newspaper, sip a coffee, you know.

He smirked, tutted and looked me down. Grey Baker's boy, over-sized jacket to my knees, baggy trousers pinched at the white socks, and winkle pickers to kick it all off.

-And what are you supposed to be? What is this?

He gestured to my whole look.

-What's what?

-This style, this weird get up? What the fuck is all this?

-Weird? Na, just the way I dress, the way I am, you know.

Just then a couple pushed past us into the café. He a huge quiff, greased pencil moustache, suit, workers boots. She a huge bouffant, red lips, short light skirt, flowing out.

-What the hell is this place?

-Just...

As he goes to enter, we hear his men down the street. They have a couple with their arms behind their backs.

-Take your hands off me!

A couple of guys drag them.

-Just leave me alone.

One guy takes the butt of his gun and smashes into the bridge of the woman's nose; the man shuts up.

-Get into the back of the fucking van now!

The officer smiles, takes a last drag, looks at me, smiles again, chucks the fag into the gutter, stands back slightly looking at the café, brushes his suit down, nods, smiles again, gets into his little black car and leaves.

I went back inside.

On stage a four-piece were mixing it up. On the bouncy floor the usual outsiders were jerking and popping each other. Be-boppers, Soulers and Cab Cats. White shirts, braces, trilbies and brogues were twisting pink dresses, glimpses of blue knickers and stocking tops. I walked to the bar and got the Rasta in a dickie-bow to pour a gin thing and roll a little doobie. The place was rocking.

I necked my drink, looked around and slipped behind the bar. The Rasta held up the cellar latch door and looking round again, I jumped down.

I knew I had been watched, so I didn't bother to knock. Inside the room was red brick and windowless. A bar in the one corner, a whole printing press, computers, stencils, bits and bobs of spares in the other. And everywhere reams and reams of paper. Copies stuck to the walls, piles of old leaflets on the floor.

-He was a bit inquisitive?

-New guy, from out of town obviously, never heard of us.

-He won't be the first to come sniffing around, and if they do, good, keeps them off track.

-Nice suit by the way.

-Ta, got it down by the docks, but where did you get that shirt?

They were admiring my new, paisley patterned, purple and blue fifties wide collar, baggy cuffs number.

-Tailor round the pipe, tunnel 7. You know him? Eddy. Gave him some old photos from the Forties, and he came up with this.

-He got any more?

-Yeah he knocked up a few like, get down there, man, he'll sort you out.

-Anyway, gentlemen of fashion, we have more important things to get all pumped up about.

We have a shipment of medicine coming in tonight, and we need to move it through the sewers. We'll get it there by cars and barges in the early hours, but we need some help from the rats to move it through.

-But we have the meeting tonight also, Tunnel 3 anti-evictions.

-I know, mate, what do you think these bloody leaflets are for?

I checked the leaflets out.

Organise to fight

Stop the evictions

Save our homes

Usual stuff: advice against arson attacks, how to barricade, how to disable diggers, same old.

So, I was off to see the rats.

***

The flyover came to a halt, suddenly in the middle of the sky the journey ended.

Other roads criss-crossed, highways on stilts.

Underneath blue and green plastic canopies, covering wood and corrugated dens. Stretched out from the protection of the flyover, buttering up the banks of the trickling river. From the dens, little pipes puffed tufts of smoke. I stood on a bridge road, it looked idyllic, comfortable from afar; some may even say romantic.

Underneath, ants hurried around, busy ants hurrying for life. Squeezed together, huggling together, fighting, no not fighting, utilising space, everyone trying desperately to cooperate with space. All the warrens of the camp lead to the centre trickle, follow the trickle to the huge centre pipe. Big enough to drive a bus down, but there are no buses here, only trickles of a river lost and a people left.

Down the tunnel was the high street, a warren on little stalls, a warren of life. Kids running in between legs, choppers smashing down on flapping chickens, men heckling, haggling. Others whisper.

Everything is there; to buy, to exchange. Smelly food, bemused puppies and kittens, even little yellow and green birds in badly soldered cages. Cheap rag dolls, expensive fake games. Piles of monitors and radios, shack after shack of phones and disks and cards, and panels and solar and battery banks of every kind. And furniture stacked high and people mending, fixing, welding, sawing.

And wires, mountains of wires and computing boards and men with huge glasses moulding and melting.

I came to the end of a leaking tunnel, wires were sparking, and there were not many people about. There was a huge metal drain cage on the floor, the water running to god knows where, there were a few smaller tunnels going off in the distance, some not lit, some barely, I took the left one, and followed the little graffiti rats marked out half hidden on the skirting of the walls.

I follow the signs and come to a hatch on the floor. I do the secret knock and it opens. I climb down into the cosy den. Kids are on settees, sitting on high cupboards, kids are everywhere in fact... in the far corner upon a high stool upon a high desk littered with tins and boxes and kettles and needles and draws of paraphernalia, sits king rat. Dalfi as he is known. He is older, but thinner, he sports a grown out blue Mohawk and the rats sit by him and admire. They pass him stuff, stolen stuff, anything really, jewellery and electronic shit mostly. He inspects then measures the amount he deems fit into a needle and a list is made into his ledger; he is a businessman. Pervatin mixed with opiates known as a high-low, both addictive both full of shit and made in factories somewhere underground. That's why the rats all look skeletal; they didn't eat much or sleep much everything was for the fix. A smother as it's known. One drug kinda cancels the other out and you get this weird massive high but you're chilled about the whole thing. Heart attacks are common and withdrawals awful.

But here Dalfi was king, he had wads of cash lying around no one would dream of stealing. He was King Rat.

-Mr Politician man, a rare pleasure, can I interest you?

-He nods to the needles.

-Not right now, and no smother... I'll take some opiate for later on though.

-Some things are hard to change huh?

I had been a rat.

-What do you need from me? From us?

-What makes you...

-No one comes down here except to smooth or cos they need something.

-A favour.

-But of course.

-I mean on top of the deal to move the stuff tonight.

-Ask away.

-I mean a serious favour, we can pay, but maybe not what it's worth. But we need it for the cause and we know you are into the cause.

-The cause is life, my friend, the cause is all our lives; so ask away.

-We need a diversion when the eviction takes place at tunnel 3.

-A diversion from what?

-We will smash the diggers up but we need the police and so on occupied.

-A dangerous situation then?

-The type you like.

-We will think of something.

***

Two days later I went to see Mama Rita, the leader of tunnel 3. She was not the official leader but she led. She organised people and fought for water and electric, even organised a private security group to police the tunnels. She had influence and politicians came to pretend to listen and she was interviewed on the TV. Everyone loved her, the kids especially because now they had schools to go to.

I came to the water at the edge of the tunnels, where life was in full swing.

Big bellied men smoked cheroots and counted bills. Women carried baskets of fish and bananas and eggs. Younger girls ate ice cream cornets and giggled at strapping boys smelting iron and hammering hangers.

I push my way through. Along the walls of the tunnels are alleys, to yet more tunnels, and more doors. Some doors are cafes, hairdressers, most are homes.

Down one alley, there is a street scene played out in miniature. The alley two, maybe three metres wide, outside most doors there are people sitting, on stools, chairs, and gossiping with their neighbour, who sits next to them. And the kids scream and chase and people come and go and smoke and fart, and kiss and slap.

I pass and look in and nod and smile. Each little doorway leads to similar places of living. One, maybe two rooms, if not a proper dug tunnel then a place hacked out of the ground, the walls smoothed, the ground hard. There's little light apart from electric bulbs, run from a battery bank or hooked up to a grid, from the community electrical engineers, who hook it up to the main frame, for a small fee. Inside, there is furniture and monitors and framed pictures and cushions, always cushions for relaxing on and sleeping for some, and always a table and chairs, for the family to sit together to eat, study and work. Space shared and used wisely.

I walk for a long while, maybe a mile or so, stop in a little juke joint for a bica and a cigarillo.

-Ladies, beautiful moves, and the skirts are amazing.

The samba babes grin, we flirt for a while.

More of the same, a city within a city, the slums now almost as big as the city they serve. This Tunnel town was only one of fifteen around the city. An independent town, with its own lighting; slightly duller, but more efficient than the brightly lit streets, and free. I came to the seedier end of the town. Here were a few remnants of the dregs of the tunnel city, the druggies, the infected, and the abandoned. Here, life wasn't sweet, but the neighbours had helped them, their crimes were committed up ground, not here, here they were left alone, and helped if they wanted it. The working girls were still here, called Rabbits now; you followed them into a tiny little warren for burrowing. But no pimps down here, the warrens were their own. They even had their own bunny rabbit tee shirts now, they belonged.

Mama Rita was here doling out needles and condoms to the girls.

-Hello, Mama.

-Why, my favourite Zazous, how fine you look as always.

-You too, my sweet Mama, busy as usual I see.

-There is no rest when you run a world, my friend!

She grinned and grabbed me in a huge hug.

-Can we talk?

-Sure, let's go for a beer at Rocco's joint, it's nearby.

We said goodbye to the Bunnies who flicked kisses back at us.

Two cold ones were laid down on the Formica table and a plate of small fried fish were also placed with bread.

-On the house, Mama.

-My dear Rocco, thank you. So, I suppose you are here about the eviction.

-Yes, just to see if we are on the same page and that we are coordinated and what not.

We have a big demonstration planned through the city in the morning and then we end up at the tunnel entrance. It will be hard for them to break through so many people.

-Well, that's what I wanted to see you about, we have another idea.

-Am I going to like it?

-I'm not sure yet, I'll give it my best shot and we'll see.

She ummed and took a big swig from her bottle.

-The rats will create a diversion.

-The rats are in on this, I am already worried.

-They are with us all the way, Mama, don't worry. They will take the police away from the entrance and then we will come in.

-To do what exactly?

-To disable the bulldozers and trucks and what not.

-I want no violence towards the workers.

-Mama, we will inform them nicely to leave their vehicles.

-No heads busted though.

-We will try not to do that, they are workers after all, some live in the tunnels themselves, if we threaten they will do as we say I'm sure.

-I want the minimum of violence; that can only be used against us by the media.

-I promise.

She smiled and sat back...

-Well, well, the Zazous have a plan; my little man is growing up! Rocco, two more of your finest please.

We clinked bottles and sat back smiling.

***

The bulldozers lined the entrance, backed up by trucks surrounded by police in helmets and long sticks.

Nearby were the police trucks and cars. Suddenly one car exploded. And from around the back of shacks little rats ran and threw petrol bombs. The police ran towards their burning vehicles and were met by pelts of stones; rats running everywhere, appearing one minute and disappearing into the warrens the next. The bulldozers stood alone, only the drivers and the foremen were left.

We walked up to the foremen and opened every door and asked the men to leave their posts, if they did no one would be hurt. Most left, a few refused and were dragged down from their seats and given a kick on the butt to send them on their way. Then we set to work pouring sugar into every petrol cap. Order was restored more or less; the rats had hit the road. The police came back along with the foremen and some of the drivers.

-Let's get this thing fucking done; shouted a captain.

-You men, get up into those cabs and let's flatten this fucking shit hole.

He ordered his own men to drive when he saw that a lot of drivers had run off.

None of the engines started and the huge ground of marchers and demonstrators cheered, as the TV cameras rolled to film the embarrassment.

After talks with Mama Rosa and other civic leaders the government had to compromise, they came to an agreement. They would spend money on improving the tunnel slums not dismantling them. They had to, they looked bad, and the world had seen the news on the net. The rats went back to robbing and injecting.

We sat in our café and watched the jazz, now and then getting visits from the cops, but they usually left after smashing a few things and roughing up a few punters.

And now and then guys in blue suits sat and smoked and listened to the jazz and sipped aperitifs. Just trying to catch on to the vibes.

Thieves' Market Labourers

The man in the trilby, braces and a tonic blue tie puts his arm round Grandad like an old mate and takes out a pair of scissors.

- Call that a tie, sir? Here, this is what we do with a tie like that!

-What the...

-That's what we do; now take that off, and here we go... Now, that is a tie, ladies and gentlemen! Now, you can have one of these beauts for three quid or two for a fiver.

I laugh and wander on, taking another bite of my beef and oyster pie, huffing steam into the chilled air, admiring our ties.

This is our patch.

Through the rough knocked up stalls selling crockery, past the vans auctioning off bags of chops, and slices of tripe.

Shoving closely down the Lane, pushing by duffle coated grandmas with fading head-scarfs and blue rinses as they jostle to get a hand up for bargains. Past stony-faced Irish guys in donkey jackets leaning, on the steps, black beers balanced on the green window-sills of the local.

Blowing past pastel saris, gleaming teethed ladies with pink head scarves selling rolls of material. Passing the van selling Jamaican jerked chicken and peas, blasting out some dub, dripping hot sauce and dreadlocks.

-Come on, ladies, I'm not asking ten pounds for these three joints, no, I'm not asking seven, I'm asking five quid. And I'll tell you what... here, Terry, throw us a bag of sausages. Here, three fifty for the lot! I'm selling me soul here, people. Come on, darling, you know your old man's going give you some loving when you serve him this lot. Am I right, ladies? You know I'm right, girl.

He winks.

The bloodied white-aproned men start doling out bags of flesh and grabbing cash from flapping hands.

Grandad winks, I smile back.

That's how I remember it. Back in the day. All changed now though hasn't it?

Well yeah, and no!

And I don't mean all changed now though in that 'back in the good old days' kinda bollocks. I would say moved on, rather than changed.

Some stuff for the better, little bits lost.

You walk past the Bolivian shop selling candles and religious tat; past Mexican hairdressers coifing up the full-bodied ladies' hair; past the exchange office, offering help with forms for Spanish speakers; to get to the bleeding pound shop. Now, you go to the shopping centre for a bit of lunch, bloody nice lunch mind you; Ecuadorian ceviche and Peruvian empanadas. Followed by a Brazilian coffee, lovely!

Yeah, it's changed. I love the newer style markets and stalls don't get me wrong, and all the different foods and that, but the old London style is disappearing a bit too much, not the new guy's fault.

Let's just say not disappeared exactly but relegated a little.

I take it all in though, loving it all, remembering it all. My streets, our streets, gone, changed streets, but still mine.

I pop into the bookies, place an accumulator on the Columbian liga, and then rush round the corner to the site, just before the end of lunch.

***

I'm a labourer, proud to be one actually. Proud too of where I live, a little corner of London, where life ain't changed that much. Well, it has changed an awful lot if I think about it, some for the good, some not. I try to not get too sentimental about it, I love change, and I love the diversity, just wish we could hang on to some of our old ways, know what I mean, some things have gone for good and that's a bit sad. But gotta embrace the new, and I do.

What makes London beautiful! The mix and the new! Always been a city of change, London; a melting pot like, and I love it for that.

I've always worked the sites since leaving school, with no qualifications of course. Followed me dad into the trade, and it is a trade; don't let anyone tell you different.

Wanted to be a footballer obviously, but after getting a trial for Charlton, I busted me knee. Used to play in the

Sunday leagues, but now I only turns out for the Queen's Head sometimes on a Saturday, when I don't have a hangover, which is not often these days.

#

We grabbed a load of canvas bags and hooked up some lights and went down into the underbelly of the hospital.

The manager, the gaffer and the old foreman standing over the hole.

-How much is down there?

-It's bad, real bad, could take us a while.

-OK, well, just get on with it then.

They really wanted to go down but they couldn't squeeze their fat suited arses down there.

We all smiled, and crawled through the foundations. It wasn't possible to kneel it was so low, but you could lie, and drag stuff. The dust was just bearable, the whole point was that we could keep the job going; we could keep our contracts going by hiding down here. At the end of the day we quickly filled the bags with hard-core and general shit and emerged looking battered and shattered.

We spent our day sleeping, chatting and taking the piss.

And me reading Memoirs of a Woman of Pleasure.

I read about Victorian orgies to a load of casual labourers.

Why? Cos I got pissed off with all the tits in the newspapers in the morning. All the comments and false boasts and the cut-outs on the wall of the shed.

Some uni lecturer I met at meetings lent me her book.

-Fuck me, and this was wrote when?

-1888.

-Good job we are down here, with this babby's arm poking out the pram!

I was their leader. Their shop steward. Got voted in cos I was really interested in doing it; to be fair I had only taken the job to get a chance to be the shop steward.

I stood on a platform of yeah yeah, of course I'll get the holiday pay in and I'll get all the safety stuff sorted, no worries; basically all the day-to-day shit done.

But I was honest with them; I was interested in the politics too even if they weren't. I wanted to get into that branch meeting and fight for stuff. My grandad had been a union bloke, on the old docks, my dad too, on the sites, he was in the Labour party too, made branch secretary. I don't hide my politics; I get it out there, get it said. Fucking hate the Tories, big business, the establishment, even the royals, though I kept that one under wraps a little, the guys still held a little something in their pants for the Queen. But, the guys support most of the stuff I fight for, once I explain some shit to them. They get it, most of it.

To be honest they love my rants, always peppered with humour, and the more outrageous the better.

-It is an English tradition that we execute Kings called Charles. It's my dream...

'Ladies and gentlemen, tonight live from the new Wembley stadium, the beheading of King Charles the third.'

***

-You should come down the common on a Sunday.

-I don't know, mate, Sunday league again!

-Mate, you could do with losing a couple a tonne, and cut down on the drink a bit. Do ya the world of good.

-Cheeky bastard. Alright I'll come down and have a look.

I went down the common on a Sunday.

There was a carnival atmosphere down there; felt like a bit of South America had de-camped to South London. Columbians, Argies, Chileans, some Africans too; from a mixture of fucked up countries. Kids were running everywhere, ducking under trestle tables laden with Tupperwares of mixed beans and ripe tomatoes, luminous avocados, soaked floppy peppers of red, yellow and green. Big bellied guys with aprons and baggy shorts and greasy quiffs stood and sweated and smoked and used what looked like over-sized clown tweezers to turn ropey steaks and splattered chickens on knocked together smoking tin bins on shaky legs. People were laid out on patch-worked quilts; most were smoking, all were nattering, giggling and shouting, gesturing widely and tucking into the top spread.

But games were being watched and yelled at too. Three games were being played enthusiastically but slowly, this was the beautiful game, not a rush and push Sunday league; turns were applauded, tricks gasped at, nutmegs laughed at.

-Maricon!

I shook hands and slapped fives. Got stuck in defence. I got stuck in as usual, committed myself. And I think my getting stuck in was appreciated, in fact complemented their delicate skills. And a few times I was pushed in the face for a tackle, got called all sorts of Spanish shit that I laughed off. The guys on my team stuck up for me though.

After, we sat and drank a few beers; chatted about the crap teams in London, especially Arsenal who most of them seemed to follow for some reason; they are still laughing about the hand-of-god goal too.

***

-Take this mate.

-What is it?

-It's about the union, your rights and all that.

-We've been told not to have anything to do with union.

-Yeah, I'm not surprised.

-We could lose our jobs if they even know we speak with you.

-That right? Even more reason to read it then, don't ya think?

The whole of the old docklands was office space now. Financial headquarters, IT companies, PR brands and advertising start-ups.

And where there's offices there's shite, and people needed to clean up the shit.

I wandered up there around eleven, me and a few other union guys, some off the sites, some from the local government departments, couple of posties. The City of London with its well-heeled army of analysts, brokers, dealers and traders doing their business in the gleaming tower blocks and offices. Working the day shift. We were there to try and recruit, try and help these poor fuckers get a better deal, a better deal for the night shift.

Off the trains they flooded. A supporting cast of thousands. Latin faces, African faces, some Eastern Europeans, thousands of 'um. An army scraping by just above the line. Caterers, cleaners, maintenance and security. Working the night shift. In the same buildings but in another timeline. And as the last of the movers and shakers stagger to a diner with food on slates and snorts in posh bogs, the hunchbacked ants take their place.

-Union, mate.

-Union? What is this?

-Trade Union, mate, workers' organisation.

People were afraid to take leaflets.

-Sindicato?

-Sindicato? Yes yes! Si, yes, Sindicato.

-I am Sindicato, back in Chile, Sindicato.

-Well, look it's on here, come to the meeting, on Sunday, at the Latin league, you know the Latin liga? On the Common?

-Common?

-Clapham, many Chileans there, big fiesta and footy, food too.

-OK, but I think not many will come, they don't speak so well English, like me.

-Yeah, shit, yeah not as good as you, mate, well, tell them to come anyway, for the food if not the footy, day out like.

-Yes, I come, I try to bring others.

-Great, but no worries, if only you come you can tell the others later on.

-I am Chico, you?

-Gary mate, nice to meet you. See you Sunday.

Chico came to the footy. I introduced him round. He was happy to see South American faces, they were happy to see him.

-Bloody politics, all the bloody time. Can't you guys give it a rest? Talk about something else.

-Like what? Women and drinking? Maybe where you're gonna score the next shipment?

-Funny! Like we are all fucking Escobar.

– Politics is life, my friend, even your life.

-I would have thought you Chileans had had enough of the politics, man. This is Europe, brother, we don't need no politics here, man; move on, bro.

After the games the Chileans loved to rant about politics, the Argentinians too; it wasn't politics for them, it was just real life, that's what they were talking about, just real life.

The Columbians, Costa Ricans and Africans had better things to talk about.

-We can't escape it, my friend.

-Yeah, yeah. I'm off. I'll leave you to it.

A few more cleaners came along. And we needed a meeting to try and coordinate things a little more; we soon realised that upstairs in a dingy smelly room of a red-bricked pub was not gonna cut it here. So, we gathered in a corner of the Common, with grilled chicken, stinking fags and bottles of Quilmes.

-So, we leaflet our guys and then the other offices.

-You've gotta get enough of your own guys on your side, then the numbers will impress.

-Yeah, and in the meantime if you can get enough of your guys to agree to join the union, we can bring in the officials, good blokes we know, and we can have a vote to join, then the union can sign you up, and once that's done, we can represent you when negotiating contracts, safety and hours and that.

-The money might be a problem.

-It's just a token amount, fiver a month, sixty a year. You have to pay to join up to make it all official like.

-But people have so little money as it is.

-I know, mate.

-Listen, I am not a cleaner but I have been listening to you guys over the last few weeks. Most of you know me; I'm part of the liga, one of the guys who started this bloody thing. You should do like we did. I think we can hold a dance, a celebration, a fiesta.

-I don't follow.

-Well, people will come to a fiesta and maybe join up but if they don't have money, we will raise some of the money from the fiesta see? And then some people who really can't afford to pay but wanna join can join for free? We can put on some food, some Latin bands, and dance. Charge a small entrance fee, and for the food.

-Who will come?

-Who will come? Why Latinos, hombre! They love a fiesta, to dance, to drink.

-I can ask one of the restaurants to lend us a function room for free.

-And we can ask the workers themselves to come. We leaflet them first about the fiesta; then they come along and get all the information about the union.

-Also, that way no one gets into trouble, for doing union stuff at work, well not yet, not until we have a big number interested.

-My friends, I believe we have hit on something.

***

I make my way to the dance after a pint in the Castle.

Pushed down the bottom of the Elephant, behind the shopping centre, round the back of the viaduct; the artisan decorated stalls of the hipster markets give way to rickety stalls and wonky wallpaper tables.

The thieves' market; an old market, a market for locals, with history, and banter, and cockneys and Latinos. There's a guy selling old buckets, and a guy that mends them. A guy selling old glasses frames and he can fix them too. A guy with an eye glass inspects old watches. Medals mounted, and postcards in cellophane. And they sit there happily nesting in with the South American bistros with tables under the arches.

Near by the old iron works factory is now a three-tier drinking, dining and dancing Latino den.

***

The fiesta was a great success; of course, it was, what's not to like? People had a great time. I danced salsa with Maria Dolares, and wow! Could she dance, me not so much but you have to get into it, and I loved it... not like I normally do, standing at the bar drinking until I have enough courage to approach someone by which time my words are slurred and nobbish. But apart from the good time the recruitment drive was a great success. Many people signed up and then after we held another recruitment meeting and signed people up who wanted to join but couldn't afford it. By the end of three months we had hundreds going into thousands over the whole of London, not just the city. Every big company had out-sourced the menial services. Hospitals, lawyer firms, telecom companies; all with a hidden army of moles; riding the morning trains if they can afford a card, or cycling on knackered old bikes or just walking, heads down through the drizzly darkness; not seeing just getting there.

-This is too much.

We are at an emergency meeting by the cleaners of the offices of a lawyers' association; a kind of trade union for god's sake!

-They are bullying us, squeezing us, if we speak out we get threatened, and they have decided to cut our break time by fifteen mins.

A bottle blonde Latino woman stands, she is not emotional, but stiff with anger.

-You sit on a train, and you see people who are earning more than you... This is a very expensive town. We have a people who are unable get a travel card, that can't put food on the table for the kids. There are people who can't come to work because they haven't got the means to come. We must make a stand, enough!

-I call for another demonstration.

-The thing about the demonstrations is they're very empowering to people who feel hidden, who feel ignored.

-Yeah, but now we have friends, we have our union; the community, the Campaign for a Living Wage group has said they will lend support too, the time is right to strike.

-Strike for what?

-You serious? We should push for a guaranteed living wage.

-But the demonstration was a success.

In March, cleaners had taken part in their first public demonstration. They took action in support of their colleague Miguel who was suspended after he walked out of a meeting with management because there was no union representative there. Recognising this as an attack on their recent unionisation, cleaners and unionists and the local community came out for a carnival like demo. All the kids from the local kindergarten wore 'We are all Miguel' masks with his face on at the demo. And there was even a majorette display in the street. Miguel was swiftly reinstated. But now they are attacking from another angle.

-Yeah, but we need to push on.

I stood.

-Look, the thing is this company, like many others, as well as the bullying, the intimidation, the attack on hours; well, as well as that they have tried to eke away at you through attacks on meal times, break times as well as pocketing staff's holiday pay and unlawful deductions in wages.

There was a flurry of discussion; of people standing and mouthing off at each other, arms flailing everywhere, fingers jabbed, heads flicked.

Chico from the football slowly stood up on a chair.

-Hombres!

People waved their hands for people to sit.

-Shhh!

-The thing is, hombres, the real thing is that they can afford to pay us, their management had four million pounds extra bonuses this year. And we, we deserve, no we demand a wage that lets us live as human beings. This is all we ask. But they won't give us that opportunity. A living wage is all we are asking for. Is that too much to ask? I don't think so. So, enough already. We must strike. We asked them nicely but they have no heart, so now we must force them to be nice. We must strike and strike now until our demands are met. We demand to live!

-All those in favour?

A sea of raised arms.

The Horizontal Bop

I stood at the back behind the cross-legged crowds.

I watched the short woman with the red bob stand and address the floor, turning around as she spoke, making sure everyone looked into her eyes.

-What we need to do is just stay here, just stay here and create something, create lots of things. We need to use the space. That's all. We build an alternative by using the space. Only then will they change their policies.

The seated ones waved their hands above their heads.

I raised my arm.

-Just speak!

-OK, sorry. I understand what you are saying and I agree with doing all those things, but let's be honest they are a bit useless.

A waving down of hands showed they disagreed.

-All the occupying of space, all the creating of happenings or whatever is great but where's the strategy? Where's our demands? We have no end goal...

The bob bobbed in...

-That's just it, if we get all bogged down with electing this and that committee voting for meaningless motions, wasting time in ironing out tactics and ideologies, empty calls on bureaucrats to do something. What's the point? It always ends nowhere, gets us nowhere. Our fight just fades away like so many old lefty campaigns in the past.

Frantic waving of hands. I shot my arm up.

-Just speak!

I put my hand down.

I needed a beer.

The cops on the door behind the barricades let me through, I went to Harry's bar round the corner from the council building.

There were a few other chefs there from nearby restaurants and work canteens and some construction guys.

-Alright, Chef.

-Chef.

-What's your poison?

-Draft Ipa, cheers.

I took a long pull.

-So, what do you make of it all?

-Seems disorganised, but hey they have a new way of doing things, interesting times.

-Load of bloody students.

-They are suspicious of us.

-Not us as such I think they are weary of the trade union officials. But basically they are there to support unionists.

-They have a good reason to not trust our fucking full-timers though.

-You got that right.

-They have sold us down the fucking river enough times.

So, maybe these kids have a point, I just can't see how we are gonna win.

-Yeah man, we have gotta be more organised.

-I think so too, but let's see how things go; we can't knock their spirit and organisation so far.

The red bob came in with some other occupiers, they obviously needed a break too, though they all had phones glued to their ears.

They sat at a table and some had coffee, most Cokes, and chips.

Big Barney, the grill man at the Chicago diner got upset.

-F- fuck's sake, Harry, give us two pitchers of IPA and a load of glasses, would ya.

He shuffled his fat arse between the chairs and plonked the pitchers on the table.

-Guys, if you come into Harry's bar and wanna stand side by side with union guys you drink. And we pay!

Cheers!

We all moved over and mingled talking about the occupation, the lack of leaders, the demands, the whole horizontal thing. We argued but in a good-hearted way. We expressed our old-time labour views, and shared stories of solid pickets, organising workers and sell outs.

Feeds sent news jumping around the room, news was relayed fast and furiously.

We were amazed. We peered at screens, gave our opinions, got quoted. We were let into a whole new world. We watched the struggle and the fight and the slander before our eyes. These kids took it all in, dealt with it swiftly and effortlessly.

Bam, blog updated.

Flash. A new tweet explosion.

Bullshit. Another politico interviewed.

Thumbs moved fast and drinks were downed.

The kids got more done, more solidarity in that bar than we could in a thousand boring meetings.

The Trotskyite chefs stood behind the kids, and I looked down the line of faces, and I swear there was a smile and a beam of proudness on every weary cook, every battered labourer. And they got us involved, they asked our advice, they told us what the hell was going on, we came alive to it all.

Bob. What about the cops tomorrow?

Me. Don't worry about them, well handle them, we've got bricklayer guys on the front and sous chefs at the back.

Bob. You're kidding right?

Me. Not really, but it's not all chefs and construction workers; we have some fire guys and bin men there too, to lend some muscle.

Bob. But no violence right, we want to be peaceful.

Me. Look, I can only promise we will not start shit, but if shit goes down we are ready, no offence but we ain't going be sitting down getting our faces gased.

Bob. You're prepared for violence?

Me. Let's just say we have some experience with this sort of thing. We have been on enough picket lines; we know how to deal with shit.

Bob. But no violence right?

Me. Sure, hopefully not.

We had a few more drinks together and I asked about herself.

***

We stayed in the state building for over a week, surrounded by a ring of cops, but no one moved. The cops hadn't been paid either so were quite sympathetic and the horizontalists fed them and watered them and chatted with them.

But all good things come to an end. The Governor stopped apologising on the TV and said that the rule of law and the workings of the state must go ahead however much people didn't like it; these outside agitators, as he worded it, were here to disrupt the democratic process. The new measures had been voted in democratically, people had voiced their opposition now it was time to get back to running the state.

The cops came at 9pm, when people had had some food and were chilling. They bust the doors down and started dragging people out. We put up a fight but this was no picket, not a fair fight. Just an invasion and an evacuation. Heads were split, limbs broken. But they cleared the place.

We met again in Harry's bar.

-You see where no violence gets you?

-We had little choice in the matter but the world saw the violence of the cops, and we came out of it in a good light.

-We fucking lost! We got our arses kicked and we lost the occupation.

-We didn't lose. We have an organisation now, we have contacts, the fight doesn't end here. We have other tactics lined up, other occupations, other protests. And we have you!

-Us?

-We have the union guys now, who can protect us and yes, when needed give us a bit of muscle!

She grinned.

-We might need some action too, some strike action to up the stakes.

-You see, that is what I am saying; we didn’t lose we won.

The Casual Sun

Four days a week for fuck all!

Hit snooze.

Just for the money, sad really.

I know that, but gotta be done.

I chew stuff over grabbing five more minutes... I'd love to get into food somehow down South. You know, just working in a café even. I'm not a bad cook neither thanks to Nan and Mum; all I have left of them now. I loved the whole vibe when I was a kid. I used to get dropped off at Nan's work, in the huge kitchens, always in awe of the foreign fat chefs with their long hats and bulging bellies, they frightened me a little; one with a single gold tooth amongst battered brown ones. But they saw it as their goal to feed me, they loved my nan... amongst the bustle they plonked me long glass vases of fruits and shades of off-white creams and ices and hundreds and thousands and a spoon as long as a shovel... and hot bread, gold butter dripping, and plates of steaming meats with gravies, mini portions served just for me... a wonderland.

Brrrrrrrr! Six o-clock, tick-tock.

Running the snooze now.

Whack!

Ciggy, take a shit, grab a peanut butter sarnie, put on me hard clothes; dusty donkey, bobble hat and hobnails and head to the stop.

***

-Mark, late again.

-Shit man, the bus was late.

-Again? Always something. Final warning.

I nod and smile, sign in.

Yeah, go fuck yourself.

-Mark, you're on track one today.

Shit, not the rolls!

And here I stand.

Fit it in, switch on, feed the sand trap, and watch the strain.

Follow the clock, fifty metres; off, cut, heave out, heave up, slam down.

String wrap-around, knot tie, pull, cut, wheel up on shoulder, stack.

Ten hours a day.

Stops for tea, arf hour for lunch, my magic box and juice.

And just to relieve the boredom sometimes we throw a match in the bitumen; and we stand and smoke with folded arms on the corner of the smoking warehouse and watch the fire-trucks arrive.

* * *

Just enough to get by but never ahead.

Enough to pay the B&B, well they say B&B but it's just a hostel really. I have a box, with a thin wonky bed and a tired mattress, a wonky wardrobe and a two-drawer bedside table with a chair next to it, a sink and a painted-up window. There is a kinda bench thing with a one-ring stove and a cupboard to store my grub; the condiments sit on a stool.

I don't have much; work clothes and one change for casual and one for best; some books and my phone, to keep in touch! And my condiments!

Love me food; Mum used to take me to work with her, with the army of casual waitresses shipped in to hotels on the edge of town... me sat in a corner, a terrine of roast spuds and puddings and a boat of gravy to dip into. He's just a kid, but I looked, in awe! Black bras, stocking tops, bare thighs, black skirts and white aprons, and arses and bellies and giggles of all shapes and sizes. And lewd shrieks and glimpses of free pink tits and knickers of pastel... forget Lord of the Rings... this was my forest of enchantment... Don't know why I'm thinking about that, as if working in a bistro is gonna be like that, but you can dream.

Wherever I go I take me little blue travel bag of condiments; salt, sugar, pepper of course; various little jars of jellies and pickles, but my herbs and spices are my babies! Rosemary and thyme for my French casseroles, basil and marjoram for various pasta; garam masala, sweet noble and turmeric cover other journeys. End of another shit day, fresh veg out, chicken marinated, reggae on the phone. I chop dirty allotment mushrooms, slice some plum tomatoes, tear some leaves and disappear in a vapour bath of garlic and thyme to a backing track of roots and Toots.

***

They're all the same, don't matter where you are.

Could be a Blackpool back to back, an old mining village, a London estate.

Same room different shithole.

Same old mind-expanding monotonous work.

Just done three months in Wales.

Months of rolling sheathing felt, warm beer, soggy fish suppers, net porn, gristly pies and dampness. My only luxury is a decent delicatessen or farmers' market or something, somewhere. I usually try and get some local veg and a little Italian sausage, or a nice cheap on the bone cut for flavour, and load it all up with a simple chicken-bone stock and wine and tomatoes and condiments. Soon as I hit town, I hit the hardware store for a big pan, I mean a big pan; and then I stew.

Apart from a few beers my food is my one touch with luxury, comfort... If I've got some decent grub I can get through the grind; at work and in my cells with a streamed film.

***

Trying to save enough for a flat deposit somewhere down the lane.

Somewhere nicer; maybe by the sea. Down South though, with the sun. Not the seaside in the North with the factory outlines and pink paper floats.

That's my plan; make my way down to the sun, move down steadily, saving on the way. Down and out through the places of once proud communities; now only nest homes of the stuck.

Miners' towns with heroin support groups.

Seafront penny arcades with skunk pushers in shell suits, and dusty kiss-me-quick hats.

Industrial towns wracked; larger, kebabs and fights around sleepers in boarded up pissy doorways.

I left cus there was fuck all. Fuck all going on, fuck all chance.

In my town they didn't open hipster bistros or retro shops; we had a greasy cafe and Poundland. And no one came to open a call centre, a warehouse; we had no start-up handouts.

There was a poor, ready-made force... but why take work to them when you can get them to come to you?

Nothing opened, all got clamped down.

So, I left. I was lucky, nothing to hold me there. Mum's dead now, sisters married off. Dad just a shell, locked in a routine of TV re-runs, frozen dinners and cans, lottery tickets and pub on dole week.

So, I left to follow the work.

Warehouses to stack, sites to carry and factories to grind the wheels.

Early starts, long days; monotonous harvest for the very bored no chancers.

I stood on roofs in the snow chucking blocks to other chapped hands. I stood on stacker trucks handing boxes to other sliced hands.

I stood in lines in the rain to get tickets and reflective tops and hard hats to protect against fuck all for a hundred quid.

To the sun!

***

-But why?

-Whadda ya mean why? Look, if you don't like it then fucking do one!

-But it's fucking dangerous, man!

-So what?

-So what? Are you fucking kidding me? Someone could get hurt.

-Like I said if you don–

-Surely this is against some kinda law, guidelines, I mean Christ on a fucking bike.

-Look man, I don't set the rules, I follow um, whatever they maybe, and I tell you guys what the fuck to do.

-I know that but...

-But nothing! This is the job, you don't like it don't fucking do it, easy as!

-That's not the point. I need the work and fuck me I do the work, I just wanna do it safely like.

-And I'm telling you this is how we do the job round here.

-Fuck it!

I jump down the elevator shaft.

Six floors of debris. Dust and wire, split wood, metal and hard core.

We pull, we strain, we heave, we smash; we eat dust and batter our bodies.

We take a breather and smoke.

-Man, why they throw this shit in here in the first place?

-Well. Look at it this way if they hadn't we wouldn't have a job now would we? Think about that.

-Shit this country's fucked!

Re-build a fucking hotel, I mean tonnes of homeless people around and loads of run-down places that people exist in and what are we doing? Building a fucking posh hotel?

Started here with an agency as usual, but guys left after a few days cus the grafter gangers from London worked them to death. So, they didn't ease off they just upped the cash offer, no agency, cash in hand like.

And now with this cash flow the sun was rising up over the horizon.

But this work, man, it's tough as fuck. I am making a big stew a day now, where it would usually last three. These fucks squeeze you, everything you do. Push ya to the edge. You carrying two two-metre chip boards up twelve flights, they scream one more. You stack twelve breeze blocks on a barrow, they bung on six more. You strain, they squeeze out more strain. You scrape till your shoulders cry, they wring a little more energy out of them.

I pack a lunch to soothe... pears and a goat's cheese, mini salamis, a decent savoury flan or pork pie, always a frittata, and some salads of available leaves and pulses. But with this work I am supplementing my taste buds. I have piles of sandwiches... pan-fried chicken and salad and tomatoes if I can, but also cheese and pickle, and peanut butter; and I am going for a full English with the guys too, a second breakfast after my poached eggs at 6-ish; and then a greasy burger in the afternoon for fuel.

Not sure how long I can keep it up for to be honest.

I mean, I love the money but standing here, body set at full volume, on top of six floors of shite, well. And my food bills are rising as I need more fuel.

***

-Was a time when a site like this would have been closed down. Union would have been in straight away.

-Yeah, now we have more health and safety bodies and there's more unsafe shit than ever.

-Yeah yeah, back in the day, fucking unions.

-Fucking unions fucking everything up.

-Whadda ya mean unions fucking everything up?

-Yeah, if the unions were on this site it would be much better.

-We wouldn't have a fucking site if the unions were here.

I take a last bite of my bacon, brie, and onion chutney sarnie and dream of the waitresses, and smile at the guys.

-Ain't no union round here now.

***

-Fucking thing moved; you feel that?

-What you on about, shit moves all the time, it's fine.

-No, no. This was different. Didn't you feel it?

-Stop whining, it's fine. Look, a couple more sacks and then we'll fuck off round the bookies.

-I don't know, man, feels different.

I start hefting the bags out of the chute and onto the floor entrance. Jump up and stack.

Suddenly...

Brmmmmmmmmmmmmmmmmmmmmm!

A thunder shoots through the building. The walls shudder, pieces break off the ceiling onto my head and then a vibration thunders up my leg into my heart, which jumps a vault of panic through my soul.

I run to the shaft.

Dust clouds.

I wave through to look.

No hard core, no wires.

-Johnny, Johnny!

The rubble was gone and so was John.

The Fabulous Jackie Buree...

I stood there putting on my purple lipstick, in front of the mirror in the hall above the phone. I was waiting for some shit to hit, I breathed in deeply and combed my hair and adjusted my miss-match of thrown together hand-me-downs and H&M chic...

-Err breakfast...

-Err, make it yourself.

-And... and this house is a fucking mess and look at the kids; they look a mess too.

Here we go!

-That's cus I'm on strike.

-I know that... on strike from the factory, for equal pay... not on strike from here like!

-Ah yes, I wanted to mention that. As of this week, we are also on strike from this shit; one day a week... from housework and child rearing, and while we are at it, on strike from picking up after yous!

Shit... I waited for the backlash.

-On strike from me, why?

Jesus Christ, this is gonna be harder than I thought.

-You have to ask me that? So some of our guys realise what we actually do. Not only do we get shat on from a great height at work we have to come home to be shat on again!

-I help round the house.

-Do you? Do you really... well, let's see how you get on for a week.

-Where you off to then? The kids need to get ready for school!

-I'm off to do brunch then onto the picket line... you sort um out!

I had a lump in my throat but quickly grabbed my fake fur coat, tied the blue scarf into a bow on top of my head, slipped on my motorbike boots and flounced out the door.

I strode with my head in the air, past the purple rinsed brigade at the bus stop, past the builders who stopped to stare a little, I ignored the whistle...

I strode down the road towards the bus stop... me, The Fabulous Jackie Buree!

Me and the girls met in Café Bonhomie... We ordered avocado on toast and muffins and banana breads; and flat whites and lattes... and got stuck in, yapping as we lapped.

I loved my girls... Tania, a heavy drinking Saturday night shagger of lucky but frightened men. And Melanie a single mum who packed a Jamaican punch in her mouth and took no shit from the wasters who hovered round her, though she always fell for the worst of them, who left her in bits in the end.

We had all been sacked. Sacked for talking to a woman's website.

We had exposed the harsh conditions of the computer motherboard factory. Long hours, short breaks, hazardous fumes from the materials, burns from the soldering irons. And short-term contracts and no union.

And the job had always been shit but recently things had got worse because of more and more unrealistic production targets being handed out.

We were working too fast, taking too many risks and not getting enough breaks; and the stress levels were affecting everyone... tiredness, and extreme irritability. And I saw depression set in on quite a few faces.

Also, we were expected to put in more overtime, which didn't go down too well at home obviously, though the guys enjoyed the extra cash.

Instead of stepping in most of our men just bitched about the house and the kids being neglected!

Us three had had enough... over wines in the local we planned to do something, we weren't sure what at first, but we read shit on Facebook, we had liked women's group pages on Facebook, and we read, when we had time; when we had five minutes to ourselves at the end of the day. When the kids were in bed and the old man watching a Champions League match on a Tuesday or Wednesday.

I got a glass and me smokes and surfed, baby! I felt in touch with the world for a change. And found out stuff, interesting stuff.

We got in touch with a woman journalist from a women's action group website. We met the journalist in a wine bar and gave her all our grievances... She wrote an article and it got passed around online and eventually it got discussed in a Guardian article... that stirred up the shit I can tell you!

So they sacked us, three women, when they discovered who had leaked the article.

So, all 136 women had walked out the gates in support and we weren't even in a union. And now the fabulous three sat in meetings with the same management, along with other striking women.

-We want an end to piece-time production; we want meetings about realistic production targets.

-But we have to make profits and meet order targets.

-By pushing us and pushing us, and now look at where that has got you, now you have no production.

-We also want proper break times and better staff facilities, better toilets as well.

-And showers and rest rooms and better food choices from a proper canteen.

-We are all working mothers; we need proper food not some baguette from a machine.

-We want a proper in-house canteen, not a big thing, we know some women in the town who could provide us with the service.

-They do great soups and salads.

-And don't forget the cheesecake.

-Ladies, ladies. These all seem all a bit mad, these demands don't you think?

-Not mad, no! We are women, you employ women and we want a better and different way of doing things.

-Also, we want reinstatement for the fab three and union recognition.

- Regular sit downs and pow wows... slowing of the production pace and regular breaks and better facilities... that's all.

-We'll get back to you.

The suited side gathered their files stuffed their briefcases and left, in a bit of a huff.

The media got more interested; cus the women spread the dispute, to a strike at home. They got interested in the day off... local women's groups and local women workers took up the cause... all were ready for the day off... Women's organisations spread the word about the day off throughout the country.

The Day Off event organisers got radio stations, television, and newspapers to run stories about gender-based discrimination and lower wages for women. The event soon garnered international attention.

The company was taking a battering not only from the media and the bad publicity but from men... men everywhere who were not looking forward to the day off.

-But, Jackie... what about picking Jane up from gymnastics?

-Timetables on the fridge.

-And shopping....

-Food's in the supermarket, you know where that is right? Recipes on Google. I'm off out...

-To a meeting again?

-Kind of.

In the pub, the meeting was over quickly.

-So, we just stay on strike until they cave, and we have a day off every week so our husbands appreciate us more... all in favour... aye!

-Actually, I would like to raise the possibility of a permanent strike at home...

-Let's not push it... our demand on the firm may be granted but the stuff at home might take a longer fight.

They all laughed, wolfed their gins down, grabbed their bags and coats and headed for legends... Ladies' night... strippers.

The Rubber Tappers and Panthers Social Club

Groups of ragged men stood around arrivals. Big hats, dusty boots, laptops and crates fought for space. They slapped backs, gripped hands and welcomed the flyers off their bi-planes. The small bar was crowded. Tables stuffed full of bottles of imported whiskey; floors stacked with duffle bags.

They stopped for a second, all stopped. All turned their heads as a small dark man in a small suit walked through the vestibule, next to him a taller man, tanned but not dark, with chinos and khaki, not a suit, strode, with a wide grin just visible underneath a wide panama.

The eyes followed them, and the murmurs started up.

A big man, belly popping out from under his designer tee shirt waddled over, blocked their path. He looked them in the eyes then spat on the floor in front of them.

'In the dark of the night, under the bending trees beneath the soft call of the cricket. There may come panthers, to rid the jungle of rodents.'

And spat again.

The two men passed and were taken to a pickup truck and driven away. In the back, they shared a cigarette. The truck bounded along the red bumpy tracks, and the fires lit up the forest, the glow seen in the distance. The glow went all along the jungle line. The smoke at intervals took an age to drift off to galaxies. The road went on for miles, the fires for centuries.

***

It was dawn, and the heat was waking up. Chico's father shook him.

-Chico, come on, it's time to go.

He yawned and stretched and reluctantly put his shorts on and went into the large room.

His father laid a flat omelette on a wooden plate. Sliced bits of fruit and broke some hard bread. Chico ate, drank some water, dunked the bread in a little goat's milk, went to the barrel and swilled the top of his body. He put his tee shirt on, sheathed his machete, put his pen and old exercise book in his knapsack along with more omelette and cake, and a tin of something; took the bag of goods and, barefoot, began his hour-long trudge through the jungle.

Down the well-trodden tracks, he skipped, he knew all the pathways, needed no map. He knew all the friendly snakes and spiders, how to avoid the unfriendly monkeys, knew what traps to look out for.

Eventually, he came to a clearing. Not a well-kept clearing, the jungle was encroaching gradually. In the middle was a small raised shack, with a little veranda. Outside a barrel for water. A few scrawny chickens pecked the dust. Chico called out. No answer. He stepped up into the hut. A few dirty pots and pans lay strewn about, bits of tappers' gear and mountains of newspapers and magazines, on a table there were more and piles of pens and notes of scrawl over tatty pages. And on the side of the bed on another table were various radios, of all sizes and shapes, with bits of wires and valves littering the place and underneath boxes and boxes of batteries.

-Eduardo, it's me, Chico!

-Is it that time already. One free day and I have to bloody teach you.

-Shall I put the coffee on?

-Do you need to ask? And pour me a Cachaça too. Did you bring food?

-My mother sent omelette, pork and beans and some sweet cakes.

-Good, put the pork and beans in the cooking pot and we'll have the cakes now before they go stale.

I sat and looked at a newspaper open on the table, dated only five days ago, we had managed to get some up to date stuff recently. Eduardo got up and in between scratching himself sank a few shots. I took the steaming pot off the paraffin burner and poured a bowlful for him. He sat, found a scrunched up pack of Al Capone menthol cigarillos, stuck a bent one in his mouth and searched for a match, I lit it for him, and with a big pull, he felt right with the morning.

He broke the cakes into his coffee, sipped, sat back and dragged some more.

-What you reading?

-About the crash.

-Source?

-Sao Paolo Daily.

-Analysis?

-- Liberal right-wing.

-As we are on the subject we may as well tune in.

This was Chico's favourite thing, listening to the world. They moved their chairs near to the table and twiddled with the Roberts radio dials. Radio America, with immaculate Portuguese.

"The coup is not a coup in the traditional sense, in the revolutionary sense; it is a coup for democracy. A coup for freedom... a cou..."

-Any surprises?

-Not really, we should expect nothing else.

Eduardo had walked into our family clearing one morning. Shabby, unwashed and clearly suffering from lack of food, and he looked exhausted. He asked for water and after he had drunk and tried to wash the grime off, we offered him food and a floor to sleep on. He took both eagerly; wolfed chicken, rice and fruit down, then stripped, washed with water again, lay down and slept for two days. He woke and joined us outside in the dusk; my father poured him a beer and gave him cigarettes.

He sat and drank and smoked and I could see him change, from a tight little tense rabbit, he unwound like a snake after squeezing his prey to death. I could tell he was glad to talk again, glad to be unwound again. He asked my father questions, got answers and then gave us more of his story.

-He don't say much this kid, but he sure as hell pays attention.

I was sat open-mouthed, chin in my palms, eyes wide, as this adventurer told his tales.

-I came through the jungle over the border to escape the troops. I had been over there to escape the military after the coup here, and now the military are over there. It seems that here is a bit safer at the moment.

He dragged on his cigarillo and smiled.

-I was imprisoned on the island after the last coup.

-What did you do?

-I was an organiser; I recruited people to the union, organised stoppages and strikes. When the popular government got in, I organised even more. On strike for more money, better conditions, we shut down loads of places, took over some. Then the military moved in.

He had escaped from the island. Helped by friendly fishermen and union guys he moved over the border. Once there he took up mining, tin mining. Again he organised and agitated strikes and occupations. He helped build a left opposition and then the cats came in the night, but he had already left.

He stayed with us for a few weeks, helping my father, learning to tap. Then he took over an old tappers hut deep in the jungle, on its own. He liked me and offered to teach me to read, he could see something in me; a fire to learn. I loved to listen to this mystical man. A man who had seen the world.

***

'In the dark of the night, under the bending trees beneath the soft call of the cricket. There may come panthers, to rid the jungle of rodents.' And spat again. They let the two men pass, finished their drink, slapped hands and filled the pickup truck with valuable wares and headed off. In the comfort of the air conditioning, they smoked Insignia Reds. The truck bounded along the red bumpy track, and the fires lit up the forest, the glow seen in the distance and on the faces of the men who didn't even notice it.

Soon the trucks turned off the roads and entered cutback wild. With fences and gates and long sweeping driveways, with horses and fruit trees, and a named sign.

At the ranch, the kids ran to get presents.

Pandas and skates, dresses and fake pearls, drones and tablets.

Kisses exchanged. The trucks unloaded; the wives' arses slapped.

In the huge living room with a bar and antlers over the fireplace, and painted family portraits, fur rugs and a couch like an Arab sheik's covering half the room, the men sank whiskey and Coke from crystal, while the women went to scold the cooks and the children to hide away, with their trinkets.

***

A few days later in a country hall.

-Gentlemen, gentlemen! If we could have some kinda order, please!

They were all men, well apart from Ma De Mella, who didn't really count. Flanked by her four brick-wall sons, she took her place at the top table; regarded as one of the main men. Had put two husbands in the ground and rumoured to have left many a ragged-arsed kid fatherless. On all the tables in the converted barn, platters were laid out large. Bursting birds, spider crabs and dripping red T-bones. Mountains of loaves, a few choice wines and brands of Whiskey; the drink of the ranchers.

-We all know why we are here. Once again, we are asking you to dig into your pockets. Things are getting stirred up, things have to be done, measures must be taken. Our organisation...

A small dark-skinned man, in a light blue shirt, nicely tailored, open to the belly with only a wisp of hair in the centre of a flat chest, moved forward from the side.

-Money? Of course, you do not even have to ask, just come and pick my pocket whenever you need to. But I am fed up of wasting our time and energy, fighting elections, organising meetings, stepping aside! Give me the word and I will solve these problems, me and my sons, and a few good people we know.

He smiled at his sons, looked around at the room, eyes wide, head nodding.

-Yes, you know what I mean. I will settle this shit in the traditional way. I will tear these fucking rodents to bits with my bare fucking teeth!

He was tense now, he mimicked picking up a small animal and ripped it apart furiously with his mouth.

-No more... will these vermin stop the progress, rob my family of money, stop us from making our living!

He rose four inches in height, he breathed in through his nostrils which widened as his whole face tensed and he spat... "Taking the food out of the mouths of my children! Just tell me and the job is done! No more talk!"

Half the room applauded and some cheered. Half looked on, serious, looked around at the police chief, the lawyer, the newspaper owner, the state governor. Looked around and wondered...

***

I grew up to tap and to organise. I became active in the union as Eduardo had instructed me to. I started local but I was a good speaker, again something Eduardo had taught me. Later I started going further afield, regional union meetings and so on. I never got to be a top official, my uncompromising politics saw to that, but I had the support of my fellow tappers and was respected enough as an honest guy to be able to push my way some way up the union ladder. Our union grew strong and with links formed with activists from down south, and new collaborations with the local tribes we became stronger. We were able to negotiate for special reserves and we got money for schools and clinics to improve the lives of the users of the forest.

But still, the ranchers never gave us a moment's peace. They wanted our land for their cattle, and their friends wanted the wood, they could see dollars in the forest; we saw only our lives and livelihoods.

They had the police and the local courts in their pockets of course. And they planned actions to just turn up and bulldoze an area they wanted. Who was there, or what was there; they didn't care.

So, conflict was inevitable.

Then, a new president got elected. A man who cared nothing for the environmentalists, a man who could see profits in the basin, a man who ignored the green lobbies; a man who basically gave the ranchers and the loggers the green light to get on with it! Get that forest down and get the dollars flowing! I saw them at the airport one time; myself and Eduardo were coming back from a meeting in a city. A few words and spit were exchanged.

***

We had organised to meet up. The union guys, the tribes, the activists from the city. The ranchers and loggers were taking advantage of the lax control of things in the basin by the government. They had taken to taking any bits of forest they fancied, whether tappers relied on it or people lived there. They even came for protected areas. We had no other course of action; we could see that; we had to stop them ourselves.

We met up where we knew the diggers and flatteners were parked up, where they would start cutting. Information filtered through.

We came in large numbers and the day they went to start their work we came out in force. At first, we talked to the drivers and pleaded with them not to flatten. Some stepped down and joined us; others were dragged down by the more angry members of our organisation. We placed trucks and trees and then lines of people in the way, any obstacle we could get, living or not.

And for the most part, we succeeded, we were too many and the drivers gave up. Other times hired hands came and fights broke out but still, we stopped them. The militants took to sabotage under the cover of night. And when the hired hands got sticks, we got sticks; the police stood by watching from a distance as yet not willing to take a side, not openly. And as yet no one had used arms.

***

One night outside in the cricket-filled air I sat with Eduardo and a good man from the union, a regional leader; a man who never compromised. He was not a big man in size but he was in passion. We talked of the future, of how to organise and how we would react if things got more serious; if the police got involved, or the hired hands got armed. The activists in the city were doing what they could to try and pressurise the government to act, they used international organisations and news outlets to spread the word of what was happening, but the new president cared little for international NGOs and liberal organisations and even the world forums. He was a businessman, a populist and saw only the opportunity of making money for the country by using the Amazon.

We drank freezing bottles of Antarctica and chewed on grilled steaks sat on the veranda of the knocked-together wooden shack called a restaurant. In a little village; dirt roads and loose dogs and samba on tinny radios. We heard motorbikes roaring around nearby, stopping and starting, but took little notice. One came past and slowed and stared at us. We got a little worried. Then another came from another direction. We stopped talking and watched. A third bike came out of an alley, the engine revving at full pelt the rider at full throttle. This bike had two men and the passenger drew a pistol and as they got near... he opened fire. We ducked down under flimsy tables and chairs. People in the bar ran and screamed or ducked and wept. The bullets pinged in the air, like a mosquito flying past. I felt one near my ear then felt the shrapnel of wood from a table hit my arm. It lasted only seconds but it felt like an age.

And they were gone.

We groped around the floor in the dark looking for each other. I was OK. Eduardo was bleeding from the leg and Armando the organiser was laid flat on his back a hole smoking in his chest and blood pouring from his mouth.

We checked him; he was dead.

The police came and took statements but we knew it was a waste of time.

We knew who had done it; well, who had ordered it. And we knew that now we had to be more organised, more careful, this was the fight for our lives. We knew that now in the dark of the night, under the bending trees beneath the soft call of the cricket. There may come panthers, to rid the jungle of us. And we knew we had to be ready.

Snogging with the Anarchists

Down easy street, you flout, reaching for angels in the trees.

You bow to the dripping chickens on the outside wall of the Los Caracoles rotisserie. You ride on down tiny winding streets, carried along on a waft of wood smoke escaping the Anarchist pizzeria. You sail past the giggling Barrio Chino transvestites to your loft space to chill before hitting the Martini bar; and then an exhibition, with champagne and canapés, before dancing uptown to touring black DJ's trip-hop. And on the way to chrome apartments with key cards, in chauffeured sharp cars with guys with beards and drainpipes who run app start-up companies, you stop off at the chocolate croissant shop; and with warm chocolate dribbling from the corner of your mouth, and white powder on the edges of your nostrils, you take a mouth of floppy hipster cock.

***

I come to rest outside a corner café, still with pot-shot marks from the civil war in the crumbling façade. I drink Cafe solo and check twitter.

Sorry to say but from tomorrow the offices will close. Our stock has crashed and the receivers have taken over. Thanks for all your efforts, Dolores. Best of luck. Matt.

What the fuck, that scummy arsehole.

What the fuck am I gonna do now? Shit, the mortgage!

Over the next few weeks, I scour the city looking for the power-skirt HR jobs that were everywhere two years ago. Now, nothing. The offices are gone. Whole new chrome and silver blocks locked up and abandoned; the vibe and loot have vamoosed.

Eventually, I manage to find a waitress job in a cool gastro cafe in Graca, purely because of my looks, if I'm honest. I had worked in bars when I left school, to help my mum muddle through before the bottle took her completely; I was useless at it.

I try and take lunch in Gaudi's park, on a bench that looks out over the once blossoming city. I read 'No one belongs here more than you' and cry into a soggy avocado and prawn bocadillo. I ride my motorbike back through the streets in the early morning as the bilingual water-men spray the filth and heat of just one day away, again. I park, steal some bread off a step, as always, and climb up to my safe haven.

-Another beer?

-Just a coffee. Café amb llet.

-What you reading?

-Lluis Xirinacs.

-Never heard of him, any good?

-Never heard of him? He's very good. A very important Catalan writer. It's about his life: writer, composer, went to prison for his beliefs; a true Catalan.

-Sounds interesting.

It doesn't really, but he is cute.

-I recommend him. He writes with love and passion. I'll lend you the book after I've finished it.

-Great. I look forward to it.

Damn cute!

I smile, turn away with a tray and flick my hair. I glance back; see if he is checking my arse, he is, so I wiggle it just a little more as I weave in between chairs back to the bar.

This is not my first glimpse of him; I've served him a few times before; tanned with a short quiff, and smartly dressed in drainpipes and loafers. Seems a bit trendy, money trendy that is, but like I say, damn good-looking and I can overlook the jumper tied around his neck.

After more flirting at the café, he eventually invites me to go for a few drinks after work, and I play it cool, I don't jump his bones straight off, which makes a change; in fact he never really hints at all towards the bedroom, which is why he intrigues me I think.

I know he is a bit of a snob, well a lot of a snob, but I am attracted to him and he wants to treat me, shallow I know. He lends me the book, which is as boring as hell. A bit too religious for my liking, a bit too serious. Banging on about Catalan this, Catalan that. Get over yourself!

I dress for the theatre after a meal on a rooftop, shake my booty in a split frock after in a snobby club. We sip Martinis overlooking the waterfront; all his treat. Which is what I need right now. We kiss and I let his hands inside the split skirt.

He invites me to his family finca for the weekend. We all drape nets under the almond trees and batter the branches with long sticks. The place is gorgeous; an idyllic painting of life outside the city; a hilly piece of dry land laden with sagging trees and bushes, with an ancient stone farmhouse with cool thick walls.

After a morning of battering, we all sit outside at a huge table with crisp white linen laid over it. Tabarded overweight women drizzle oil from on high from thick green bottles, their bingo-wings flapping the steam from plonked racks of lamb. Long crimson peppers pop on the grill: wheels of bread are ripped, orange butter scooped; dusty cava, majestic cognac, wise reds, unruly leaves mixed with dandelion heads. I don't like his family much, all a bit toffee-nosed, but I really enjoy the luxury of it all, and at least they are a family.

His father, a prominent doctor and businessman stands and toasts.

-Mira, you see all this beautiful food? It is Catalan food! Not Spanish, Catalan. You see the faces around this table? They are Catalan faces! This land rolling before your very eyes, this is Catalan land, the finest land in the world!

Yeah, yeah, I get it, Catalan!

I knock back a brandy.

We eat gloriously for a few hours; I chat about mundane stuff, telling the women what they want to hear... babies... yeah, family? Of course... Young people today... yadda yadda... playing down my work problems, money worries, I lie a lot. I laugh at the right moments, and nod and smile when I disagree. I drink long, but carefully.

We two stroll together when the others sleep.

-It's lovely here.

-As my father would say, behold the Catalan beauty.

-He is a bit mad about the whole Catalan thing, don't you think?

-He is proud, I am too. I love Catalonia, I am sorry to see it being destroyed.

-I love Catalonia too, and being Spanish, but you know...

-That is another thing, another discussion for another day.

We snog on a knoll with a view. And finally I let him screw me; face pushed against a derelict Catalan wall; Catalan knickers around my tanned Catalan ankles.

My savings get eaten away. The waitress wages barely cover my living expenses. The still rich tip badly. Eventually, the bar lets me go. Like I say, I wasn't much of a waitress.

I take a job in a local disco in Barrio Chino; not one of the trendy cool bars that charge a fortune to listen to Manu Chau because he is actually sitting in the VIP suite. This is for the less well-off, the hawkers and drug dealers, Arabs and back-packers, unemployed and low wagers. I work all bloody night, work with abuse, knife fights; I stand in a constant puddle of filth. We snort heavily cut speed in the cubicles, to keep going. After closing time in the early morning, I go for a few wines and breakfast, sharing the moaning about our shit lives. Then home, and try to sleep.

Eventually, the bailiffs come, I manage to grab some belongings; luckily I have minimalist tastes. And I have never been one for hoarding mementoes. My fucking alcoholic mother left few photos, and most of the furniture was gone well before she was.

I move into a friend's flat, down the darker narrower side streets further away from the turning chickens on the rotisserie.

My friend Lola is an artist, a good artist, and also beautiful, with deep almond skin and a dirty blonde bob. She never has to dress up to look good, she throws something on; a tight bundle of bohemian tinder-sticks. She goes to the top of the Ramblas and sits and waits. And a stubby pot-bellied man always comes along. The 'art-lover' stays the night on the stained mattress on un-shiny wooden floors, and takes a painting in the morning, and leaves a little money for groceries, and art.

I learn to paint.

My flat has gone but not the debt. The interest alone is more than I earn or paint for. I ignore it, and try and do the best I can, hoping something will come along. I keep seeing Milan, he is my connection to the old life, to the good life, I once had. He is a bit boring and conservative and luckily I don't see him that often, but when I do, I get treated nicely.

Me and Lola, who's always been a bit of an anarchist, start going to shared space events, I need some kind of social life. Lefty students' squats; disused, derelict buildings. Street theatre shows, free gigs, cheap thrills and beer for local youth pushed out of their own city's cultural life; a place for migrants who were never invited. A gathering for the disaffected and down-trodden, and lost.

I had grown up in the crummy back-streets. I had known the winos and the druggies, the working girls and the immigrants. I knew them and hated it all. I had planned my way out, and now I was right back down there with them.

But things have changed, I see a change. These spaces were once the realm of the unwashed, the arty leftie types. The very people I would have twirled my vintage skirt away from and sniggered at from behind my small-batch single-origin bean latte. But now, lesbians in wellies giggle with single mums; bearded owners of thrift shops chat with jobless car factory workers, scooter riding graphic designers smoke a spliff with a family escaping a war. And for once I see not the badass side of the underbelly. I get to see and meet, good people, friendly people, people who are trying to do something to help themselves; let's be honest they have to. I meet people who have lost everything, no work, no home, no family. And when I hear their stories, I cry my eyes out and get them another plate of veggie stew.

I am still seeing Milan, when he has time; he runs one of his father's businesses, selling property to foreigners. He is away a lot, showing them round old properties in the countryside or new flats in towns, or near the sea.

He takes me dancing to the old dance hall, in the afternoon, with cheerful old couples dressed up in mothball suits and fading frocks, and still in love, still trying to cut-a-rug. We dine uptown, served meals on wood, crammed in tightly next to prominent figures, in sharp suits armed with prominent figures in tight dresses.

He is very political, and angry. And he makes me a bit sick going on about the bloody foreigners and the bloody lazy poor people. I put up with it I think because he is something to hang on to, a way back perhaps, to a better life. But I know I have to be careful, not let him take control.

In the end, me and Lola fall out, I can't make my share of the rent, I lose the shit bar job, and fucked one of her best arty clients when I was smashed.

A few of my new girlfriends are squatting in a building in the old neighbourhood, the thought terrifies me, but I check it out, it isn't so bad, in fact, it's better than Lola's place, and free.

-Why would you move into a squat?

-What other choice do I have?

-I've told you, I can pay for an apartment for you.

-And I've told you before that is not gonna happen. And besides, it's really pretty cool.

-Please don't mention where you live to anyone will you, you know, when we go out?

-To your snobby friends, you mean? To your high and mighty family, you mean?

-Just please don't.

-You know, fuck you and your pathetic friends and family.

-I'll see you soon.

***

The police hit the squat in the morning.

Bang! Rush, push, voices, stamping, chaos.

What the fuck! Who the fuck are you?

Grabbed sheets, pulled hair, bare arses.

Grab your shit and get the fuck out!

Slap, smack, kick, flack.

-Yeah, and fuck your mother too!

***

Now, I share a room in a left for dead 19th-century building, not many left now; some done up, some torn down, many left to rot. Our room must have been an old ballroom at one time; it has a cobwebbed chandelier still hanging from the huge ceilings, and peeling floral wallpaper, and dust and torn cream drapes. I share a room with seven women, two babies and one child. We partition off the room with patterned cloth blankets, to try and have some sort of privacy; but we are happy to live with each other, the sharing is nice. We share the cleaning duties, and cook together, watch and play with the kids; laugh, comfort and sooth each other's souls. And I talk to people about real things; real problems. And I hear terrible stories from people who came here for a better life, people who came to escape. People who have lost or gambled everything. But also local people, in more or less the same boat. People who have lost everything; their homes, their jobs; their hope most of all. I realise, they are just like me, and I am just like them. Here, here we try and get some kind of hope back, some kind of dignity, some kind of community. And I think I have come to trust people more, and think about how others feel, more.

We start to cook for everyone living in the building, and also people who come just to eat, who are just hungry.

We take deliveries of veg from nearby stores, and cooperative farms, who donate. We scour the restaurant alleys, collecting what's thrown out, what's perfectly fine, and get handed crates of stuff from hung-over smoking chefs in the back alleys.

We play music in the kitchen as we chop aubergines to braise with chickpeas in long stews, and place cheeses and breads from friendly bakers and makers on the long tables decorated with blankets and old shawls.

Everyone sits and eats together, when possible, some pop in just to eat, in-between working, others after a hard day dealing with red tape, others from scavenging; others as there is nowhere else.

I get involved.

I go to evictions, where we try to plead with bailiffs. One time, I physically try to stop a young girl being dragged from her bed where she clings to her teddy. I get a black eye and a thick lip, and angry. We take the family and what can be salvaged of their belongings and move them into other empty buildings.

We get involved.

And maybe for the first time in my life, I feel awake. I see things more clearly. I understand more somehow.

We take over more buildings, move more families in. We get plumbers to turn on the water. We get electricians to turn on the energy. We call in favours.

I see a need to help people and in that, I see a way to help myself somehow. I need less shit. I still take a café solo in posing places uptown now and then. I try to look my best with my second-hand underground chic. I steal lipstick and scrounge eye-liner. I still like to get dolled up. I am still me.

I see Milan again, for the last time. His attitude has been getting worse and worse. And I see him for what he is now; a shallow, spoilt, little nationalist. A jumped up little yuppie shit.

I know, I know, I used him for his cash and to keep in touch with what I had lost, but I never got kept by him, I drew the line at being a kept woman, which is what he wanted to do.

We meet in the old Champagneria near the port. I remember it used to be an old bodega with old tins and hanging hams sweating into little upside-down umbrellas. My friends and I loved the place, years ago. They only served champagne, pink or white, and Roquefort and bacon bocodillas. And local people used to stop by after work to enjoy the cava and the belonging. Now it's full of a younger crowd, with labels and tablets and beards and acquaintances, and a selection of wines and champagnes, and tapas on slates.

-You are doing what?

-We are setting up a centre for refugee children, the kids need somewhere to study, to play, to learn. The old cinema in Graca, you know it? It's been empty for ages and...

He starts fidgeting and puffing through his nose.

-That is a fucking historical building, part of our Catalan heritage.

-Jesus, chill out, man! I know what it is and it's been fucking left to rot by the fucking Catalan council, that's how much they care for the Catalan heritage.

-But why not help the Catalan homeless; people need help.

- We do help them, we are the only ones helping them, us, we are the Catalan homeless, the Catalan unemployed, we help ourselves, and we will help anybody who needs a roof or a home or food in their belly. The fucking Catalan government doesn't help them or us. But people need other things too, they need education and a place to play and...

-Let them get that shit back in their own country; their fathers should be in their own country providing for their kids there like we do here. Why are the men here? I'll tell you why; they are either here to get a free hand-out or are fucking terrorists.

-Terrorists? Are you for real? These are families escaping a war, kids, women, and yes, men.

-And why do they not stay and fight in their countries?

-Not everyone is a fighter.

-Who is to say that they are not sleepers, sneaking in under the cover of refugees?

-Sleepers? Fuck me it's not a John le Carré novel? It's not 1956 Berlin, they aren't the fucking KGB; they are refugees, families, escaping a fucking war.

-That's all the bullshit from the EU and liberal bleeding-heart politicians. You believe all that crap? Well, I fucking know better than that.

-You fucking think so?

-Yes, I do fucking think so, I know so. And I'll tell you one thing I would be a fighter if Catalan was under fire not like those men who ran away. I am a fighter for Catalan, and one day, one day...

-Yeah, a fighter for who? Like your father you mean? He was a fighter for Catalan, wasn't he? Back in...

Smack!

-You watch your dirty mouth!

He pushes a few stunned tipplers out the way, I wipe the blood from my mouth and go to the huge open wooden door, lean on a champagne crate, and shout after him.

-An... and by the way, I think we should start seeing other people.

***

I come running round the corner, down off the hill. I heard the bang as I sat in the park. I saw the flash, and felt the thump up through Gaudi's bench, deep through my arse.

I come running round the corner to see the flames growing up the sides of the centre. The old cinema has started to give way. A few bodies are lying in the street, other people are bloodied and staggering, some are being comforted, some help; others scream, others shout, others sob.

And blood, singed clothes, burnt torn flesh, and shock behind watery eyes, lost eyes.

I spot a mother, Isobel. I run towards her but she stops me and points desperately at the burning building.

-Dolores, please! My child. Xaawo is inside! Dolores! Please!

I run. Two firemen grab me.

-You can't go in, it's too late, it's too late.

-Fuck you.

I punch and kick, try and wriggle free, with all my might, out of their holds.

I run.

You run, but the heat beats you back. You run but the flames light up the night.

You run but get nowhere.

You are dragged back.

-Let me fucking go. I must go in, there's a child in there. Xaawo is in there, a fucking kid!

Then I see her, under a blanket, I break the grip again and run over and squeeze her close.

-You are safe. Xaawo, you are safe. Your mamma is here too.

-My father is inside.

I carry her over to her mother and stand and look at the blaze reaching its climax. In a last crescendo, it blows; we all stand and watch.

I turn, there's a big old wall with a little blue tourist sign nearby, pointing the way up Carmel hill, to the escape of Guell. It is eclipsed by a big graffiti stencil. The outline of the Catalan flag with the face of Xirinac in the foreground, and the words underneath in big black letters...

Act of Sovereignty ! Visca Catalunya!

Six Hungarian sausages

The train pulled in, last stop on the Slovak border. I leant out, the snow was pelting down but the platform was crowded with heavily wrapped up folk. A young woman in grey pressed a wrapped package into my hand and blew a kiss. I sat back and unwrapped.

Six Hungarian sausages. Nice gesture, I thought, nice of her to come out, spare the time to come and give me something for the journey. I wiped the window and blew her a kiss. I imagined getting off, and being taken to her small apartment in a tenement and being given Turkish coffee and a shot of slivovice and huddling round her wood burning stove, and taking more shots, and then she would lead me into her freezing bedroom and we would get under the layers of goose feathered duvets and make love.

But, I was on a journey and that wasn't going to happen.

The train jerked off and we all, us men, strained at the windows and waved. Back in the couchette we all unwrapped our various presents. A smoked ham, a loaf of dark bread and label-less bottles. We produced knives and cut bits off and offered them round; the bottles following.

We cheered up, ignoring for a moment what lay ahead; a war.

I chewed on the spicy sausage, took some raw onions and my nose came alight. I swigged and my throat ignited, and I felt loved.

On our way to war. A war of conscience.

The full-on civil war in Ukraine had been going on for six months, and the anti-fascists had called for help. So, like in Spain, International Brigades sprang up.

The media had portrayed the Revolution there as a people's uprising; but it was nothing of the sort. Some reporters mentioned the Nazi influence and the platoons of storm-troopers, but no one intervened.

Only on Facebook was the real story heard. Put out by activists.

Even when fascist hordes burned down a trade union building in Odessa killing fifty people, the papers ignored the fact; that it was fascists.

So, things had gone from bad to worse, the parliament was now full of oligarchs and fascist leaders.

In Donbass, where we were heading the media said it was Russian activists who were fighting the government; cease fire and elections failed to bring an end to the war and now it was an easy split. Right wing paramilitary inside the regular army and the government, against left wing separatists.

I sank another fire water as we passed through Hungary. The train was taking the long way round, but even here in

Hungary we were worried. The Hungarian government were no friends of a left wing train.

I had dreamed of this. Had read Orwell's account of his adventures in Catalonia and had wished for this. The chance to be a real revolutionary. The chance to fight properly for my ideals, my beliefs.

-More drink?

-Sure.

-Speck?

Some guy with a big moustache sliced me a slab.

-Where you from, comrade?

-Manchester, and you?

-Prague.

-Beautiful place Prague.

-Baa! Too many tourists and too many capitalists and corrupt politicians.

-Just like Manchester then but we have few tourists but too many rich students.

-I am from Valencia.

Another guy piped up, young, athletic, well compared to me he was.

-My great-grandfather fought in the civil war.

-Really? Which side?

I grinned but my Manc humour was lost on him.

-The left forces of course.

He bit his sausage and frowned at me.

-What you do in Manchester? asked the Czech.

-Construction, building, when I was younger then I worked full time for the trade unions, you?

-Me, car factory; I also am trade unionist.

The young Spanish kid spoke.

-I was a student, but then no work, I went back to work on the land, in a collective.

I looked at him and felt old, maybe too old for this fight. I was in my fifties for god's sake! Podgy belly and bad legs and not much hair.

-What did you study?

-Political science, but it was bullshit! And then no work at all for me and other young people.

The couchette was warm now. The food and drink had woken the wagon up, and talking laughing and even singing could be heard throughout. People sat back and relaxed a bit, took more swigs and smoked; we tried each other's various cigarettes.

-Jesus, how can you smoke these?

I coughed and tried again. The black-looking tobacco was like smoking a log.

-Ah Englishman, this is nothing, I get no smoke from this stick, this is not tobacco!

-Where you from anyway?

-I am Swiss.

Me, my Spaniard and my Czech all looked a little taken aback.

-No shit! Brought your knife with you I hope.

-Yes, I know all the jokes but let me tell you we have problems in my country too.

-Sorry, mate, I don't doubt it, and you are here, so good on ya.

-You ever fight before? the young Spaniard said.

-What, you mean in a war? The Swiss guy replied with a puzzled look.

-I was a regular in the Swiss army.

Now I looked puzzled.

-But I thought the Swiss army never entered into conflict?

-We have been part of peace-keeping forces many times. I was in Kosova.

The young Spaniard was looking nervous.

-But did you ever shoot someone?

-No.

-And you guys?

We all said no, we had never shot or killed anyone. We all became silent for a moment, not looking at each other.

The Czech piped up.

-But what does that matter? We are here now and when we need to kill we will kill, no?

I shrugged my shoulders. Before I had been blasé about the killing part – I'm gonna blow their fucking heads off, man! I had bragged to my mates in the pub, but now as the civil war loomed closer up the track I realised I was afraid.

I ate some sausage.

Running with Water

I lean over and uncover the ham, take my stone-ground knife out and slice thin slithers from the sweating beast.

-Shara! Dish out the eggs.

-Turn the coffee down, Maria.

My guys are gathered round the oak table, in a little cottage tacked onto the end of the stable blocks, in the corner of the stone courtyard. Each are in various processes of dressing, some rubbing eyes, some leaning on the shoulder of others and dozing. Others are pissing or brushing teeth. The early risers are already walking horses from pens to fields.

I poke my head out and shout above the clopping.

-People! Breakfast is ready.

On the table is a black iron pan full of fried eggs; plates of sliced avocado, blood tomatoes and slightly stinking salami, all floating in olive oil. Huge crusty loaves are ripped apart and lashed with orange butter. And finally little bowls of olives and cold roasted peppers, and bowls for coffee and left-over cake to dunk.

-So, four guys are on horse duty, that's you Sajila, you Jose, and Petr and Veronica.

-We need some supplies today, so Leonel and Sue take the 4-by-4 and go round the other farms. I'll make up a list.

-Yeah, all the bushes will be arriving today, so we need to get started on the digging, it's a huge project, guys, so let's get going as soon as possible, there's a lorry load of helpers coming from town. Elvira, you supervise them OK?

-Also we have the eco-friendly spray for the olives, came yesterday so we need one guy on the tractor and two spraying. After we meet for lunch we should all be able to get stuck into the bush planting.

- And don't forget someone has to go to the cooperative collective meeting tonight, anyone?

-Don't all volunteer at once!

I had been in Spain for four years. I had come over on a boat. I paid all the money my father and I had managed to save. We worked on our small farm, me and my five brothers and sisters. We worked hard there for the family but we also studied, our father wanted us all to have an education, so we would all tramp the four kilometres to the village school through the dust. We farmed food for our family table, and also flowers, hundreds of flowers, that were collected every week, to be sent to richer parts of Europe.

We had enough to live on, just. Just enough to eat and wear clean clothes; my mother was always washing and repairing our clothes, we always looked neat. But I saw my mother go hungry sometimes, I saw her give the little ones her own bread, smiling. So, my father put some money away each week, just a little, from extra work he could get from the big house. And I started collecting after school, collected cans, and bottles and paper, to sell.

So, we paid a guy the man in the big house introduced us to, and I took a boat at night across the straights, dodged search lights in the gloom.

We made it onto a small beach, and ran to meet another man, who rushed us up the beach and through a forest of sand and small trees. We spent the night in an old farmhouse with no roof. I was sick from the crossing, and ate the last of my mum's flat bread, and drank mint tea from a dirty tin off a makeshift fire until the man came back and stamped it out. The next few days we slept in the day, in abandoned homes. We scraped together roots to eat and filled up vessels to drink. In the night we travelled over fields, up hills. We crouched when we saw lights, or heard engines. I was in the open but had never felt more closed in.

Then we arrived at our new home. We were put up in a huge old barn, with bunk beds and one shower, and a toilet-hole in a wooden shed stinking out the back.

We worked, under the plastic; mending, cutting, weeding, spraying, picking, sweating.

Long days from sun up to down, the heat was almost unbearable, I fainted a couple of times. After, we ate what we could and slept for as long as possible.

We had one day off which we spent washing clothes, cooking and sleeping. Sometimes we wandered into the village to get supplies, and would sit for a while, just a little while, and take a coffee and a chat, speaking in hushes to avoid suspicion, and dreamed of home, and tried to raise a smile, but more often we brought a tear.

The pay was low, and the work back-breaking; from the heat I got headaches, from the chemicals I got burns, from the wet and cold I got coughs, from the tiredness I got bad dreams.

I worked, I tried to save some money to send home but it was very little.

I got to know some local people; introduced by Spanish workmates. I sat and watched the football on a flickering TV in the local farmers' café; we drank a few beers as we ate free tapas, and shouted together at the screen.

After six months I was offered a job by a local guy, Joao, he worked on a small cooperative farm that had horses and olives. Run by six families, who shared the land and the work. They all lived nearby in small buildings.

He was a nice guy, let me stay in a small caravan he had on his land which was touching the snow. I tended the horses on the mountainside, and took care of the olives in the groves and sometimes helped do work around the friends' houses. The work was hard but pleasant. I shared meals with the families, and went to local fiestas, and drank wine, and danced again, and slept long.

We spent days fixing old stone walls, stripped down to our shorts, the wind licking my face as I looked out in the direction of home.

I gradually felt part of the mountain somehow, part of a family. I felt I belonged. I felt that at last the work I was doing was worthwhile; hard and back-breaking but it was for our benefit, for my benefit.

I worked for another year for Joao and the families and learnt a lot. I learned to share and work with others. I was happy, part of a community again, and I was able to help my family back home at last.

I then met a girl, a graduate from Madrid. Maria had come back to her family's village. There was no work for her in the city and she didn't want to leave, but there was nothing to keep her there, only fraying ties. She was helping her family on their small finca, nearby our own little community. Maria had a natural affinity with horses. That's how come we spent time together. She came to love the village; we would take trips up the mountainside on horseback to sit among the apple trees, sip wine. We chatted about our differences and of what we had in common. We spoke of our disappointments our failed hopes and passed olives between our lips.

***

I came from Madrid, first to visit my family and their farm. It was an escape from the city. We came every year to escape the heat of the city, the drone of the city. Back in Madrid I worked hard for my degrees, sociology and psychology. Always studying, always being pushed by my father. Then when I left university there were no jobs, nothing. All my friends were in the same fix. We had done what was expected, studied and studied, with the promise of a good job, money, security. Now the banks had wasted all the money, now there were no jobs.

I felt bitter. Bitter towards my father most of all; he had made me follow his rules, his way. But his promises were empty. I blamed him and his generation. They had lost the money; they had allowed the greed to win out. Now, what was left for me? Nothing!

So, I went to the finca to escape, my degrees worthless, but my love of horses eternal. I could feel free there. Could feel useful there, my life had worth. My father had shut up! He couldn't complain anymore that I was wasting my life away, dreaming my life away in fields of fancy.

I met Hamza; we worked together in the fields, spraying the olives, shovelling horse shit. And riding, always riding. We would go for long treks through the thin forests a little way back from the sea. To little cantinas, for a salad and steak from an outside grill. We sipped little sparkling wines and always had a jar of our olives to share.

We got a little money together and moved to Marinaleda.

One hundred kilometres from Seville lies the small village of Marinaleda. We heard the mayor was a good guy. We heard that the village had no unemployment. That everyone worked and people were given land to work, with low rents. We heard how he expropriated land and buildings long left to rot. And created a communal way of living. We heard he took over supermarkets when people needed food and buildings to help the homeless.

Marinaleda is a place where the farms and the processing plants are collectively owned and provide work for everyone who wants it. We were given a mortgage for only €15 per month.

We attend football matches in a stadium emblazoned with a huge mural of Che Guevara. Once a month we have 'Red Sundays' when everyone works together to clean up the neighbourhood. We work our little place, grow olives, breed horses. We work with friends and help others.

We have a little finca. Four old buildings we did up, with stables for about fifteen horses. There are twelve of us living here. We live collectively and are more of a family than a business. Everyone chips in; everyone has enough to live nicely. We give horse lessons to guests, who stay in the old farmhouse in the corner of our fields. Or who come from the cities for a day or two and stay in town. We harvest olives, organically, and sell them abroad and to Madrid and Valencia.

***

-Papers?

-I don't have any with me.

-You have to come with us.

-But he lives near here; he runs a collective farm...

-No papers then he comes with us.

-And me?

-You are not a foreigner.

-And because he is, he immediately gets taken away.

-We are just carrying out the law.

I sit in this detention centre now; weeks have gone by.

Sitting and doing nothing, waiting. For the red tape to be cut, for the kicks to stop, for the verbal diarrhoea to be wiped. Stuck in a no man's land.

-Get the fuck up!

-Sorry, sorry.

-I said up, scumbag.

Slap

Boot

Spit

-I am now legal here, check the records.

-We can find no records, so until then you stay here, or we send you back.

-But...

-I said shut the fuck up!

***

I sit on the roof, with my fellow inmates. With the placards and rocks. I sit and wave for the cameras, and look out to the horizon and remember and hope.

I remember one day Maria walked me on high, around steep crevices, through over-grown pathways.

At the top were pools, fresh and natural, we took long drinks.

Maria showed me what to do; I had to free up the wells, open up the drains, un-clog the stone guttering that clung to the sides of the ravines.

Let wild the ancient channels that followed at the side of sparsely beaten tracks that irrigates the life of the Alpujarras.

We had to run with the water, jog along with the ghosts of the Moorish Acequias.

This was an annual thing. Every early spring the old farmers and their young brothers, sons, cousins would all have to do it. It was like a rite of passage for young men. A way for a man to get in touch with the workings of the mountains.

We freed up the first pool, and a trickle started, I worked faster, and a flow followed. I ran.

We ran to the first blockage and kneeled and quickly threw branches and stones and leaves over my shoulders.

The water continued on. We ran after.

The water was always ahead of me. But I learnt to wait. I learnt to clean it all away, and catch the water up. I learnt to keep the water at bay; I cleared until I was ready to let it loose.

And then, after a few hours, we cleaned the troughs ahead for hundreds of yards, and walked back.

We let the gates open, and down the track we ran, with the water by our side, we ran together.

I ran with Maria. I ran with the spirits of my forefathers, I ran with my family, I ran without fear, without a border or a frontier. I ran with the breath and breathed with the beat of the mountainside.

We jogged with ghosts, running with the water.

And now I sit here on the roof, protesting. Waiting to see if I can stay or not, waiting for a bureaucrat to decide if I will run with Maria with the water again, sit with my friends for breakfast again; ride through the forest to the hilltop again and pass an olive to Maria's lips again.

I sit on the roof and look out at the sea and wait.

Kissing Teeth

Mandala walked home along the shore, his bare feet tickling the lap of the gentle waves. The sun still stood above the lake on the horizon, but would soon lazily lie down for the night.

Beep! Beep, beep!

Text

'Gt lil butr n sum oranges 4 a treat. X'

-I wish she would stop that text talk.

He traipsed back 400 yards or so, and left the lakeshore, crossed the crocodile river by way of the rope bridge and followed the dirt tracks that wound round baked clay and straw huts, and dodged kids chasing and chickens running for their lives.

He came to Tom's shack.

-Ah Mandala, a shot of powers? Or maybe a Kachasu?

-No, I am on the way home and I need butter.

-No butter only margarine. And a powers also, no?

He looks at him, then away, kissing his teeth.

He shoots.

-And one from the house.

The store owner pours. Mandala sips this time.

-Why are you being so generous?

-Can a man not treat his brother?

Suck

-A man yes, but you?

Tom smiles and nods his head.

-You joke, my friend, I know you joke.

Mandala looks at him, sucks again, and takes a sip. He leans with his back on the wobbly counter and looks out from the open front over the only tarmac road in the district, at the ragged boys kicking a rubber football in the dust around the abandoned market stalls.

-So, what's new, Tom, my old friend.

-Business is bad, my brother, business is bad.

-For you business is always bad, I've never heard you say it's good.

-And always that is true.

-Yeah, so bad! You live in that palace, with bricks and a generator and your fat children.

-Only from the will of god, my friend, only from the will of god, never from the pockets of my friends.

Mandala sniffs and sips again.

-And how is the fishing village.

-Hard and thankless.

-At least you have work, my brother, you are one of the lucky ones.

-That why your being nice to me? Lucky? I'm not so sure, I don't think having the fishing village has been lucky for us. The fish are getting fewer and fewer, my brother, those big cats from the city are draining the life out of this lake, and where does it all go? Shall I tell you? To the city, my friend.

-Business is business, my friend.

-Business is business. I'll tell you this, things were simpler when we just fished this lake for ourselves. We had our wakos and nets and ate what we caught, and sold and swapped, simple.

-Poor times, I think you forget. Look now you have money to buy things, nice things.

-Yeah, nice things, my woman wants nice things we don't really need.

Tom nods his head...Click!

Mandala shrugs his shoulders and with his bottom lip fully over his top, shakes his head.

-Huh, nice things. Give me a Kasacha.

Tom uncorks and pours an extra-long one.

-So, did you hear? There were people at the lodge.

-People, what people?

-Muzungus, in 4-b-4s, and white shirts and ties, Important. They stayed at the government inn for a few days. Many meetings.

-Really? Has anyone met them, talked to them? Why they here?

-Some of the old boys from Maya met them, along with the chief of course.

-Why didn't you say?

He slaps some Kwacha on the counter and leaves.

-Anytime, my brother, always a welcome for you.

Mandala passes a few women pounding cassava in huge mortars with large wooden pestles, and enters into the middle of four closely-knit huts. A group of men are sat down on logs chugging from white cartons; in-between swigs and laughter they shake shake.

-Mandala, sit and shake, brother.

Huge laughter all round.

He is handed a carton, shakes it and grimacing takes a long hit of the maze beer.

He wipes his mouth with his shirt.

-So, what's the story with the Mzungus at Maya, Green?

-Yes, I met them. Good fellows, big ideas and big bucks!

He toasts.

-Mzungus!

All the men raise their cartons.

-Mzungus!

They take big sups and then fall about.

-And?

-And, some guys have bought Maya, and are going to open up a volunteer charity place, or something.

-And jobs?

-Yes, they are hiring and there will be cash for other things too.

-So, no lodge, no customers?

-No, big business, serious people.

-Shit, I need to check it out.

-Mandala!

They all slug and Mandala leaves to screaming laughter.

He gets his margarine, and buys some small oranges off an old man by the side of the road. He has a brown beer at the cola store, to extinguish the last of his thirst, searching as always, for more e-way mail.

E-way mail: You send a message that-way, a guy would meet your guy on-the-way, they send a message on-its-way; that-way the message comes your-way... E-way-mail.

He makes his way back through the bush and continues his journey along the shore. Feeling relaxed now and a little excited. He hums to himself.

Back home he sits outside his baking mud hut, taking globs of Nsima in his fingers, dipping into the tomato relish, cracking a little dried fish, mashing all together before placing it in his mouth, as an orange stands nearby on a smooth rock, proudly.

He watches the lake closing down and listens to his treasured Roberts short-wave radio; the world service, the BBC brings news of Africa today.

* * *

Turned out they needed all the old workers at the old Maya beach lodge, despite the history, the allegations. Even Aron, the python killer was given a job, and he had been caught, stealing paraffin.

All twenty of the old workers were hired, and more. Hired to guide, to plant, to mend, to sew, to fix and to build. And more villagers were hired; the football team were hired to bring trees from the forest, huge trees carried by eleven men on their heads, unless one was ill, or drunk and then his wife took his place. People were paid; for food, grown or picked, charcoal makers, firewood collectors, and reed gatherers.

Brand new huts were built; trucks brought toilets and sinks from the big city. Latrines were constructed, new kitchens were knocked up, and new decking laid on the rocks.

The whole place was spruced up.

The workers had never had a toilet to use before, they went in the bush.

And equipment, new lamps, new nets, working clothes; and best of all a messroom, with hooks and a locker each.

This was no Mzungu holiday trip, this was a better place.

There is a meeting in the bar, the bosses of the volunteer centre and the original Maya workers.

-But how will we make money with no guests?

-We will have volunteers, and they pay a great deal more money to come here to work on their projects.

The group swapped sceptical scowls.

Mandala spoke again.

-They pay to come and work?

-Yes, they each are specialists in their field and we will vet, check, every project before they come to see if it is workable.

-These projects, what are we talking about?

-Projects to help the community.

-And we will get paid, bwana?

-Yes, you will get paid as employees of Mwaya, and other local tradesmen and villagers will get paid for any service they provide, but we will need your families, your friends to help work with these projects.

-And these people will be paid, our friends and family?

-No, I'm afraid not, but they will be working on projects to benefit themselves.

-But they will not be paid?

-No, but they will work on projects to help the community.

Mandala stretched back on the bench and sipped his Fanta and shook his head.

-People will not work for free, bwana, people want work for money.

-I understand, and eventually we hope that people will get paid work, will better their life, from what comes out of the projects. We hope to build schools, provide education, maybe a health clinic, we can train health workers, and gardeners trained in new methods can provide food, which saves families money, so in effect they are earning.

Mandala was a little angry.

-Nice ideas, bwana, but I see many problems, and the biggest is this... the chief will never agree to develop the villages.

-We thought he would welcome the chance for his people to develop, the chance for the people to have a better life.

Everyone looked sheepishly at each other, and lastly at Mandala to say what they all thought.

-Pay him off.

-What?

-I cannot speak badly of our chief, but I know this, he will not give up his power lightly. But money will soften him.

-We will see.

Mandala smirked and drank the dregs from his can.

-Remember what I said to you today, bwana, it may help you later on.

The meeting went on for another hour or so, and the workers left eventually, rabbiting on about all the new ideas and plans as they shuffled along the lake clasping the fresh banana bread close to their chests. And chatted with their wives in the dark, by the sparkle of the lake, as the chickens slept.

***

-You cannot buy off my villagers anymore, I won't allow it!

Manny, the volunteer, looked at the chief puzzled.

-But I want the money to go back into the village, this village.

-No, the children steal my reeds, if they know they cannot get money for them they won't steal them.

-But I can buy them off you?

-Of course.

-But aren't the reeds everyone's, they are available for everyone.

-Not here, I am the chief of all this lake, they can cut from the places I say, but those little thieves stole mine. They know which ones are mine.

Manny looked at him.

-The best ones are yours you mean.

-No more, no sales to my people.

He turned and hobbled off with his staff with his grannies around him.

Manny turned, shaking his head, looked at the line of women with kids around their feet, shrugged his shoulders and held out his arms. The women mumbled, put the bundles of reeds back on their heads and dragged the kids back up the sand paths.

Mandala had been watching of course, he watched everything. He grabbed a couple of ruffians and sent e-way mail to friends in the other three villages.

They met in in the football teams training camp. Basically a few falling down huts where the team met, got stoned and drank shake shake.

-It's easy, our women cut the reeds and your wives carry them to Mwaya.

-And we get paid.

-We share the money.

-If our women cut it too, they get all the money.

-Look, this way, we can cut and carry at twice the speed, so we get good money, and the job is done quicker, everyone wins, everyone's happy, even the chief, we keep him happy.

-Let's hope he doesn't catch on.

-He won't, he is too interested in watching that his reeds are not sold.

All agreed and passed the joint around to seal the deal.

***

The place got done up even more. The kitchen was modernised with running taps, gas bottle stoves, sinks, sealed store rooms, and a cold cellar sunk into the ground.

A new bar and eating area on the rocks. The traditional African huts were replaced by proper wooden chalets, on stilts, and proper thatching; mozzie nets bought, old ones given away, sheets and proper beds added.

Volunteers came, with projects.

The first school building was built.

A basic health clinic started, supplied with first aid medicines and equipment and knowledge, for local women. Children were treated, inoculated, de-wormed and cleaned up generally.

Doctors came, builders came, scientists and even gardeners.

Things started to get done. Things stared to be learnt, work started to be useful. Ideas became useful. Skills taught that made sense, projects started that mattered.

Organic gardening was introduced, because it made sense. Permaculture introduced because there was no alternative.

Ideas, that out of Africa are alternatives, were introduced because they were a way of bettering people's lives. In fact they were the only way; cheap logical, doable and effective. Everything made sense if it was put into the proper perspective.

***

-But we catch more.

-Yeah, but the nets are too fine, too many smaller fish are getting caught.

-Yeah, but we have enough fish.

-That's the problem right there. If you keep on catching the smaller ones eventually, the supply of fish will run out.

-But there are lots of big ones now.

-I know, now but...

A fishery adviser volunteer was starting to lose patience.

-Listen! What I am saying is...

***

People's lives got better.

New fishing methods were introduced, the small ones not trapped in the mosquito nets, so after a while the fish got bigger and there were more of them.

People worked on the community gardens, so people got healthier. And there was plenty of food. People's diets got more varied, so people got stronger.

But along with this people were also working, getting paid for bits of work. So, people wanted to buy stuff, any old stuff.

-He wants what?

Mandala was translating for Yona, a good footballer, sometime thief and full-time hard worker.

-He wants to have a sub of his wages to buy a clock. A Mickey Mouse clock.

-A Mickey Mouse clock, are you kidding? Now, if he wanted to invest in some boots, I would understand it but a clock?

-It's what he wants, bwana.

-But wouldn't it be better to buy something useful, for the kids, some books, some food even.

-He wants a clock, boss.

Some of the women took classes from the visiting health workers.

Their natural instincts for survival techniques was enhanced with proper, basic care, and healthy techniques, cleanliness, childcare. And basic first aid was taught and learned eagerly.

-Why is he outside?

-He has a fever, maybe turbolo.

-Then we need to keep him cool not buried under blankets in the sun.

-Not sweat it out of him?

-No.

Latrines and dry toilets were built and dug, away from dwellings, away from water.

Grazed knees were treated with soap and water and a tube of Germolene, a small thing but a very important one.

And schools were filled with a few basic things, blackboards instead of sticks in the sand.

Tables to sit at, books to be read and pencils to write with. And teachers to teach, local and from abroad, and methods were swapped and lessons learnt, and pupils came every day, gladly.

But the chief felt his power weaken. His people were getting stronger and more knowledgeable and worst of all they were organising and demanding things, things to change.

* * *

Thud, thud, the sound of running feet. Scuffle, thud.

The watchmen were disabled; the men went into the Muzungu's huts.

-Up, everyone!

One guy reached for a machete.

A cool guy sat on the corner of a wonky table and pointed a pistol at him.

-My friend, I wouldn't if I were you.

The men were tied up and restrained with machetes or rifles at their temples or throats. The women pleaded and were pepper sprayed. The men, about ten in all, ransacked the place. Packing everything of value into sacks and bags. Satisfied, the cool guy took a look around.

-You will stay here and not move, we have scouts posted nearby and if someone comes out or tries to raise the alarm we will be back.

He turns, sheaths his knife and walks calmly out. After a few hours some people got free and gingerly went to help the wounded, but luckily still alive, watchmen. They sent a runner to the chief so he could contact the army road block a few kilometres away. But no one came.

It was morning when the police and the chief and villagers descended on Mwaya. There was chaos and the watchmen told tall tales of their heroics. The police took statements of such but it all seemed to fade away as the sun came down and the people drifted off.

***

In Chinchete market a shout went up.

A man was trying to sell an expensive camera.

-He is a thief, a thief from Mwaya.

People pushed him and punched him. He was grabbed and he pleaded, and named others, denying his involvement. Then the crowd got angrier and started beating him with their fists; as he went down, they kicked him and then threw rocks on him, until the life went out of him.

The guns went off as people ran from their plots into their huts. Three men were running and firing backwards. The police advanced. Eventually behind a hut a policeman shot one man through the head. Another was injured in the leg in the dunes near the lakeside. The third man ran out of bullets and surrendered and was kicked and slapped back to the station but protected by the police chief; he was the son of the chief.

I Really Need to Borrow Nan's Monkey Wrench

Thursday's bin day. I make sure all the stuff is in the right bins, all the stuff that can be recycled is in its right place. While I'm there I take food to the compost pile.

I do my bit. No airplane trips this year, just a tent near Cromer on the wild East coast. We got rid of the car last year; well we got rid of one of the cars, so now we have just the one. But in the city we all have passes for the transport; even the kids take the bus to school now they are a bit older. We shop local and eat healthily, if not local then organically.

The kids went on strike from school, very proud of them. And Elena has been on some swarming actions, you know blocking the roads, sit downs in front of offices to cause inconvenience.

***

-But what are you really doing?

-Like I said, we recycle, we keep our carbon footprints low, we protest.

-The kids protest.

-Well, yeah and we support the protest.

-But, it's not enough.

My mum, the kids' gran, huffed and got stuck into her nut roast. Sunday dinners are always like this, won't be long before we hear the stories of battles of the past.

-In my day...

And there we go!

-We put up maps showing how much of East Anglia and London would be under water as temperatures soared and the sea levels rose. This was in the early 1980s. We concentrated on what individuals could do to lower their carbon footprints – by putting up solar panels, changing light bulbs, practising recycling and re-use, eating less meat, using public transport, shopping carefully and locally, and consuming less. That was thirty years ago; it has taken people that long to catch on to what we were saying back then. And now that isn't enough!

-What more can we do, we go on the marches, we sign the petitions we have changed our lives, we can only pressure the government and so on.

She was gone now; lost in a dream of past protests.

-After discovering the impact that UK timber imports were having on the loss of old-growth forests and their biodiversity, I even got involved in carbon sink campaignsand sustainable forest management. I worked with major UK timber importers to persuade them to stop importing timber stolen from indigenous reserves in South America and Asia... In my day, we really got stuck into them! When the Americans put nuclear sites up we chained ourselves to the fences, we camped out for two years, two years! The governments are not listening; the kids have the right idea.

***

Three weeks later I get a call to pick up my mum from the police station, she was arrested outside a fracking site, blocking the road using one of those locking arms things; she had been inside for two days as she refused the bail conditions.

She got in the car.

-Do you have a ciggy; I could use a smoke.

-You can have a puff on my electric one.

-Just pull into the station I'll go buy some.

She hunched as she ran sheltering from the rain under her yellow mac. She came out with fags and four cans of lager.

She got in, lit one up and took a big gulp from the tin.

-Ahh! That's better. I must say the food in the cells is much better these days, even the beds are quite comfortable.

-What were you thinking, getting arrested!

-Jesus, it wasn't my choice, I just refused to move.

-But at your age.

-Bollocks, at my age, hark at you! You sound like some old bag yourself.

-But getting arrested, what about the kids?

-Jesus, can you hear yourself; the kids are gonna be proud of their gran I can tell you, and you should be too; I am at least getting up off my arse, when are you gonna do something?

I stayed silent, she was right of course, and god I really did sound like an old biddy!

***

I was glad to hear mum had signed up for evening classes at the local college.

That will keep her busy, I thought; knitting or pottery or some such craft based activity.

I was sat reading the Observer one Sunday, with toast and marmalade while I waited for a fry-up.

Machines burned at fracking construction site.

Five huge construction machines have been expertly set on fire at major site.

There have been many protests, vigils, hunger strikes in front of that building, over the last six months after public commentary hearings, with no response from the local authorities who had allowed the pipeline to be built.

***

-Someone is really going for it now!

-So, you heard about the fires then?

-Sure, good job huh?

-Yeah, but it is really holding off the inevitable.

-But, the longer it is held off the better and more people get to hear about how

bad it is.

-But it's still gonna go ahead.

-We've got to try at least.

-We?

-Well, you know it affects us all and we are all in it, in the fight.

Over the next few weeks there were more headlines.

Saboteurs had welded empty pipeline valves, and moved up and down the pipeline's length, destroying the valves and delaying construction for weeks.

These reports went on for months. Highly skilled welders were making the valves obsolete.

* * *

-So, what is gran actually studying at night school? I asked my daughter.

-Don't know; something with metal, I think?

-Metal?

-Yeah, cool or what?

-What sort of metal, like jewellery?

-No idea, ask her!

-I bloody will.

I didn't have to wait to ask her. I heard about it on the local news. Three pensioners arrested, with monkey wrenches and blow torches at a pipeline intersection.

I Fell Asleep Under the Borrachero Tree

The boat builder finished up for the day as the sun was coming down over the bay. Renzo stepped down from his baby, washed as much of the aqua-blue paint off with his sweat, put on his trilby, hiked his Bermudas under his belly; and shirtless walked the thirty-nine yards down the red dusty roadway to Charlie Chaplin's bar, as he did every day. Under the coconut leaf roof, he pulled up a stool, got a Polar straight from the freezer without asking, and sucked hard. He let out a gasp, wiped his mouth with the back of his hand and looked around the wall-less little bar.

There was a married man with a local girl, young, in the corner; a tight blue mini skirt hugging her jutting-out bum.

Renzo leant with his elbows on the bar and observed; you could balance your Polar on that.

An old couple, a few worker guys with overalls rolled down to their waist, and a street kid in black shorts, working the grill, turning fatty steaks; waving the smoke from his eyes.

At the one corner of the square bar is Osmer-who-looks-out-from-behind-his-hand, who is chatting to himself and, looking now and then, peeking from behind a curtain. He had once been on a Scopolamine trip for fourteen days, but never really fully came back.

Renzo shakes his head.

Shitttttt, who knows what fucking trip that guy got stuck in.

More locals pitch up, it was the end of a working day for some. Young guys on mopeds stopped to chat to school girls supping sumos. A couple of office guys in ties came in sweating with briefcases and suckled gratefully from the tit of a Polar bear.

The evening wore on, and people came and conversations went. Another steak was slapped on the grill, another argument rose and wafted away on the back of the Jonron smoke.

Renzo's friends started to come. Backs were slapped and Polars clinked.

-They laid off 120 at the sugar factory today.

-Yeah, and the bricklayers are laid off again, another half-built school.

-Gas is up again.

-I know a hundred coins a jar today, a hundred a jar!

- Romeo y Julieta were up again today too. Gonna have to switch brands soon.

-I found a young girl on the ground today, kicked out of home, man it broke my fucking heart.

-So, I took her for food and a few drinks, you know, she was very grateful.

Smiles and Polar clinks all round.

-So Renzo, how is that boat of yours coming along? Seems like you have been building it forever.

Some nodded others laughed.

-Yeah Renzo, pull your finger out, boy! It's not as if you have any other work to distract you.

Backs slapped and more laughs.

-Gentlemen, it is not the sailing of the boat that is the destination but the building of the boat that is the thing.

-Words of Polar wisdom.

-The boat will be finished when I am good and ready to finish it.

-Renzo, you know it is just an excuse to get away from Alejandra and the brats.

-My friend, you are wrong, Alejandra is the very reason I plane and paint away every spare minute, every spare minute to build for the day we can sail.

-Renzo, you are a dreamer.

-Without dreams, my friend, we are just poodle moths, watching as discovery passes us by.

Again, laughs and raising of glasses.

-To Renzo, the boat builder and philosopher.

***

-There are no more orders to be had. So, we need to cut numbers and cut wages, and that's it.

Louis barges his way from the back of the crowd of angry men and stops in front of the manager.

-How can there be no production to be had? Is it because the quarry workers have taken over mining and formed a co-op and won't sell to you at a cheap price?

-The co-op has nothing to do with it; the demand for tiles is down... and...

-The demand is not down. The price on the market is low, you mean, and you want to cut production until the price goes up again. But we produce good products here.

-We have to be competitive.

-You have to make a profit for the shareholders, you mean.

-We have to run this business as a business.

Louis turns his back on the manager and faces the crowd.

-And that, ladies and gentlemen, is why he, they, want to cut our money, lay some of us off, not because there is no demand for clay products, no, it is because there is not enough profit to be made at this time.

The manger gets angry.

-Listen, I have tried to explain the situation to you, but the bottom line is this, production will be cut, only two shifts from tomorrow morning. Wages will be reduced from the beginning of next month. When, when we need you again we will put a general call out on the radio, and that is it.

He puts his papers into his briefcase and to jeers and scuffles he is led away by private security guys and other office workers.

The crowd of two hundred mostly men huddle in small groups, they discuss, they argue; no one laughs, they smoke and huff, some sit and hold their heads in their hands.

***

-So, jobs gone, money cut, just like that.

-Yep.

Renzo puts a fat Romeo in his mouth, sets a flame to it and skilfully puffs until the engine is running, and satisfied lets out a lungful and lets the smoke roll up his face.

-Shit, I never liked that guy, always thought he was better than everyone else when we were kids.

So, what now?

-I'm all for a strike.

-You would be. But what about the others, bet they're not?

-And so what of it, Renzo? What else do you propose we do? But yes, actually most of us are behind the idea. For many, it's the only chance they've got.

-Why do you care about what the others can and can't do? You should be looking out for yourself; you've always been a good worker, though always a troublemaker, might not be that easy to get work. Going on strike, you'll never win. Anyway, what do you hope to get out of striking?

-To keep jobs and money, what else do you think?

-I know you, man, you just love to stir up the shit. All that communist bullshit. Why you really for going on strike?

-Fuck, man, it ain't rocket science, it's about getting a better deal for people.

-Why do you care so much about other people, man? I've never understood you, man, look out for yourself first.

-Well, that's where you and I differ.

-You got that fucking right.

***

- We set up pickets, and stop anyone going in.

-We should have a ballot, like the union says.

-Fuck the ballot, we are here now let's vote now, if we go home and listen to our wives, to others, to the union lackeys we will vote to take the cuts. We are all here now; we take a show of hands now.

-But then they will say it's illegal, that we are not being democratic and all that shit.

-And they will print and say lies about us no matter what we do.

Louis stood.

-My friends, I will say this. No one has the right to vote another guy unemployed, no one has the right to vote away another guy's job. Not in the safety of his own home. We vote here and now. Everyone has the right to vote as they see fit, for strike action, or for the loss of jobs and maybe eventual closure. But we do it here and now; we do it honestly and democratically. Face to face.

They held the vote.

In favour; the vast majority.

Not in favour; no one held up their hands, the ones not convinced abstained.

It was clear, they wanted to fight.

***

The men marched to the gates on the Monday, a long procession, they were in good spirits. They gathered in the courtyard of the factory buildings. The men waited five minutes for the hooter to sound. Then they walked out the gates and stood looking in at the management at the windows.

A delegation came out.

-We want no cuts in wages and no loss of jobs.

-And we have already told you we have to cut jobs and wages, to make ends meet.

-Look, no one is going to work until we get guarantees.

-If you guys don't come to work we will find others who will.

The management turned and walked back inside

* * *

They picketed for a week; the strike was solid.

-So they will bring in other workers then?

-Has to happen.

-So, big pickets from tomorrow.

-It will take them a few days to hire guys and organise to bus them in.

-Where they gonna get workers from, round here?

-No, they know that won't work, they will bring them in from other towns. What we need to do is stop those buses and talk to the guys.

-They are not gonna let us talk to them.

-Look, if we have enough people there we can stop those buses then we can talk to them.

-But the union guys want us to negotiate with the management.

-Fuck the union guys. We are out now, solid, the union are just gonna negotiate a lesser loss, a few less jobs, a little less money. We have the initiative. We picket the scab buses and turn them round.

-And if that don't work?

-If talk don't stop them buses, we have to come up with other ways to stop them.

-Violence you mean?

-Picketing, through strength, and numbers, not violence as such.

-But it could end that way?

-It could.

The picket was large for the next few days.

-There's three buses been spotted on the edge of town.

-Let's get to the factory, get word around. We need bodies.

A mob got there just in time; they stopped the buses. A few cop cars rolled up, but kept to the side.

Louis stepped up onto the bus.

-Gentlemen, you know who we are, we are here to ask you to not go inside that gate. We are asking you to help us in our fight. We are asking you to support us in our struggle to keep our jobs; our families, our community ask you. Please don't cross that picket line.

-We don't know anything about anything. We were signed up to work for the agency and we have been brought here to work. We just want to work, for our families, for our communities.

-Gentlemen, we are asking you nicely to help us in our struggle, we appreciate your position, we know you need work, but that is why we need you to help us so that we can work, and live.

-Seems to me that your problem is with the management, it's nothing to do with us; you should sort it out with the management.

-I have never crossed a picket line in my life, and I'm not about to do that now.

-Me too.

Ten from the first bus got off, not much arguing and shouting. They went with Louis to the other buses, another twenty men got off.

Louis stood on an old concrete boulder to the side of the buses.

-Gentlemen! If you refuse to support us, then you are basically supporting the bosses, you are saying that you want us to lose our jobs. Gentlemen, we ask you again to not cross. If you do then you take the consequences.

The police moved in. The crowd start shouting, and moving on the buses, the buses moved slowly, a few rocks thrown, the buses pushed the line back, the police dragged people away, more police arrive. Fists fly, arms are bent up, people flung away. The buses pass.

The factory got closed; the workers fought battles with the security guards, the scabs and then the police.

Heads were opened, arms broken; younger guys torched trucks and threw cocktails at cops.

The manager got attacked and left for dead, in front of his family on a balmy summer evening, near the port.

***

The management walked away eventually. Left it to wither, cutting their losses, they took their security and files and scabs and moved on. Who needed the hassle? Shut it down and move elsewhere.

Louis and the other guys entered the compound, with no resistance, scratching their heads.

They went through the scattered invoices, and filed them back into the empty drawers of the cabinets.

They set up an assembly of workers, and their families. They realised that they had been producing a lot of waste and that that waste could be re-sold.

Dances were organised and tickets sold. Cakes baked. Prizes given out.

And all the proceeds went to the fund to help families who struggled, to help clothe kids, send them to school with their books.

They guarded the factory and took stock. Other co-ops were invited to the assemblies to lend their knowledge.

Inside the factory a kitchen was set up, and donations were collected from friendly farms and shopkeepers. People gathered every day, people got fed, children played, and meetings were held. The men were occupied driving, collecting, up-keeping the factory, preparing for production. Also, busy learning from others about cooperation.

***

-You run it? How, how the hell are you gonna run it? Run it with those imbeciles, and with whose money?

-We can do it together; we run the place anyway, what's wrong with us doing it ourselves? Everybody chips in, everyone works together. We can work with the other cooperatives if businesses don't want to.

-You're living in dreamland, my friend. What about management, keeping the books, paying the wages, buying, selling, you guys have no idea how to run things?

-That's why I am here, Renzo, to ask if your wife will come and help us.

-My Alejandra?

-Sure, she does the accounts at the wood mill and works at the town hall.

-And that's just where she is going to stay.

-But we will be able pay her a wage once we are up and running.

-Really, you can guarantee that can you? You can't. We need her job; I am telling you she is not interested, Louis.

-Can we not ask her opinion about it?

-Louis, I have given you my decision, she stays where she is, and don't even think about approaching her with your mad schemes.

-You need her job, Renzo, cus you don't work; you just scheme and dodge, and booze and build that fucking boat of yours.

-My friend, I am working every day, in my way, I put money and food on the table.

-Yeah from where though, from where?

-You work your way, Louis, and I work mine, just like we always have done. But, my friend, I don't have pie in the sky dreams. You were always a do-gooder, trying to help other people, and where did that get you? Fucking nowhere that's where. I, my friend, I live in the real world. I, my friend, look after mine and my own first and foremost.

Louis kicked the dust and turned.

-Yeah, yeah, Renzo, always your way, always the looking after number one.

-But Louis, what other way is there? I look after what's mine.

He jumps up on top of the boat and holds up his beer to the sky and yells.

-Sah-Lood! Keep on dreaming, Louis; it's what you do best.

***

-Alejandra, we need your help, we are in the factory now, we are working, well not properly but stuff is getting done, stuff is being prepared.

-You know I can't.

-I know Renzo has told you that you can't.

-And he is my husband, I respect his views.

-His views, but what about your views?

-Look, you know I would love to help, I really would, I believe in what you are doing, Louis, I do.

-At least just come and have a quick look at the books, and maybe give us a few pointers.

-I can't.

-Just a quick look.

-I'm not promising anything.

-Great.

She looked around at the work being done. She was impressed by the spirit, the community feel.

She looked through the offices and studied the books, shaking her head the more she read.

***

-OK, OK, I will do what I can.

-And what about the licences required by the local council?

-I will talk to Paulo, from the council, he helps some of the other co-ops in the area; he's a good man.

-Thank you, Ala, we need someone with a clear mind to help us here, to get things running.

-It's not for you, you understand, but I know many of the mothers, and they are worried and a little desperate.

-I know, but I thank you just the same.

-And I can see what you are trying to do here is good.

He stroked the hairs on her forearm, and she smiled and sighed a little.

-I have been listening to the men in some of the discussions and there are many who can help with the ordering, the planning and so on, but you are the best speaker, you will have to do lots of the deals yourself, you know that?

-I can do that, so long as the main decisions are still made in the assembly, I can do that, we can do business with the co-ops, the quarry and the drivers' co-op.

-I know that, but someone has got to go out and sell your stuff, you need someone to contact the buyers. You are a good talker, a trustworthy man, you should do it.

-I don't think I could face those bastards. I'm no capitalist.

- I think you can, Louis, really, and we need others too, others who will keep their head, and get a good deal.

***

-You know what I said? And you have been working with these guys for nothing.

-I know but things have changed now, things have moved on.

-I don't want you involved with a load of communists.

-They are not communists they ar–

He raises his hand, but she leans her check into him the muscles on her neck straining.

-Go on then!

He flicks her arm and walks away.

-Enough already.

-Don't you ever hit me, ever, do you understand me?

-You should shut your mouth and do as I say.

-Fuck you!

-Fuck me, fuck me? You see, you hang out with a bunch of fucking Trots and you get all fucking mouthy. Fucking Louis man, fucking Louis.

-What the hell has Louis got to do with it?

She walks over, picks up a fresh Arepa and slices avocado to go inside, she leans back against the wooden table, stabs a lone slice of cheese and bites into the Arepa and chewing, waves the long knife at Renzo.

-You raised your hand to me once before do you remember? And I warned you then. Another time and...

-And you'll what? You should remember your fucking place, woman, and not another word of shit about the fucking factory out of your mouth.

Renzo grabs a bottle and a brush and goes out the door and climbs onto his boat.

Ala raises the knife and places the cheese into her mouth, watching him through the window.

***

-So, why are you giving us this information?

-I felt it's my civic duty.

-And you want nothing in return for this favour.

-No.

-What's your interest in this meeting, why are you so interested in these groups and what they get up to?

-Like I said, civic duty.

The officer grinned and puffed on his cigar.

-No personal interest at all?

-Well... there's a guy and...

-I knew it!

The moustached sergeant leant back on his chair, crossed his leather boots and grinned at his men standing round him.

-I bet there's a woman involved somewhere right?

Renzo frowned and looked away.

-I knew it, always a woman. We thank you, brother, for the information you have given us, some people will be most interested in it.

Renzo slowly crept to the door and slinked out into the shadows.

* * *

The meeting was held in an old Indian village five miles from the city, in an old clearing was a meeting hut used by the tribes for ceremonies. Alejandra and Louis had contacted unions, co-ops, tribal groups and activists from down south. They were meeting to coordinate work between the coops and to bring people together so they could act in solidarity.

The hall was packed; people had come by buses, wagons, pick -ups; even donkeys, the groups from remote villages had walked.

They elected a committee which were seated behind a mish-mash of tables; these were only elected to help the meeting get along with business.

Shhhhhhhhhhoe...Through the window came a grenade. It bounced on the floor and swivelled round, everyone seemed to stop for a second, then Phoof! The tear gas exploded. Then came more through the windows. Chaos broke out as everyone ran for the exits. Outside there were lines of men, armed with clubs and sticks and some had drawn firearms. These thugs had been hired by the local business community and some police and army joined them, though not in uniform. They ran at the running men, smacking and batting heads and bodies. The people ran, there was no way to organise a defence, no time; that would have to wait till the next time but for now heads were cracked.

***

Louis walked with his two friends along the sand not far from their homes.

-We will meet again, they can't stop us, we just need to be careful who we let know next time, we need to be more organised about the whole thing.

-It's true that word got around very easily and quickly, it wasn't hard for the police and others to find out.

- But someone tipped them off.

As they came to the wooden wharf nearer home they saw a big gulf of smoke and people running. They ran too.

There on the floor on his knees in the dirt road was Renzo sobbing. In front of him in flames was his boat going from aqua-blue to singed brown quickly. He didn't even try to stop the flames.

Alejandra came through the crowd and stood near Louis, she squeezed his hand and he smiled and leaned into her and smelt the gasoline.

A Riot on the Quiet

From the end of the street a line of black, helmeted cops started advancing. From behind them between their shoulders tear gas was launched.

-Come on!

Black clad youths advanced, some wore gas masks, some tied handkerchiefs.

People dodged the gas and the rubber bullets, others hit them back with placards, some threw them back.

People filmed, people texted, tweeted and passed on information, arranged rendezvous.

People met up and ran, met up and chased off, met up and hid and threw and charged.

Bottles, wood, glass, cocktails.

Horses were clopping up the street, slowly at first; then charging.

People dived into doorways; people fell under hooves.

Some people strung up a rope across the street. Riders were brought down.

Three guys wait, two jump in front; the horse rears back, the third leaps and brings the rider down. They beat the man until he lies still.

People had filtered into the old town all day; sporadic groups, all following Twitter and Facebook, all busy with their thumbs. Where to meet, where to avoid, where the cops were at.

People arrived to clashes. They had come to show their anger, their distrust, they came to protest.

A small group of students had occupied their campus and were discussing.

-You are from where?

-The UK.

-You are here to support us?

-Of course.

-Why are you here to support us?

-Because your fight is our fight too.

-Sit down and don't speak.

-Can I text?

-Sure.

I took to Twitter.

I am here #revooccupy all going down. Fighting and organising.

I had travelled by train, got a fake inter-rail ticket from some woman at the socialist press. I had met a nice girl from Dresden on the train, a small brunette babe with a short skirt and docs... we had wine in the couchette and pulled the beds down and had a fumble in the dark.

I had been sent from the Students' Union, a rare thing! The FE colleges rarely got a look in at the uni dominated Students' Union. But I got voted in to travel to Czech to show our support and to report back. The five others had bought proper tickets but I was watching the money, the expenses they had given out were a good wad of dosh so I didn't wanna waste any. I might need it for more important things.

I crossed the mountains into Czech. I knew I had crossed by the look of the ticket collectors. Heavy metal locks under ill-fitting hats.

Prague was a buzzing. I wandered the streets, checked the phone, stopping for a beer at various places recommended by other activists on the red/activist pubs of Europe app.

I traced the steps of Hasek and Hrabel. The Hospodas were crowded with students, hippies and younger kids with quiffs and caps, tight baggy pants and attitudes.

It was early evening. A few protest marches had started. From various points, all heading to the direction of the main square.

-Who you represent?

-I'm a student too, not a university though from FE college.

-College, like Cambridge?

-No mate, it's like a college for the working classes, no one goes to uni anymore.

-Really, why?

-People do, but we have to pay, so only rich fuckers get to go, the rest of us just grab what we can from a college.

-And why you here?

-To show you that we support you, we are behind you and to hopefully get inspired and go back with some hopes and dreams.

I smiled at the guy and he raised his beer mug.

-So, you are protesting basically against the closing of the squat?

-Not a squat, a community centre, where we helped homeless and refugees.

-Yeah, yeah, sorry. But that's what this is about, the eviction?

-It started out as a protest against that but now it is something more.

-Such as?

-It is against our corrupt politicians and the austerity measures they are trying to push through.

-And it's mostly students yeah?

-it started out as student activists, people from the centre, then other students came to support us, and then more and more and then it spread to other towns. Now the students have been joined by normal people.

-Trade unionists?

-Some, but not as official organisations, their leaders are in bed with the politicos. But many, how do you say, normal members are here. But many people are just workers and old people too; they are finding it more and more difficult to live now.

I was busy writing notes.

-Where will you publish this?

-Most probably on student websites, lefty Facebook groups you know.

-OK, sounds good.

-And where do you go from here? I mean the place is burning, and the rioting is fierce but have any demands been met?

-I am not sure where we go from here, maybe we will occupy spaces, like in Egypt, maybe we can bring people out on strike, maybe we can stop the working of the new measures, that is what I hope for.

-And the rioting?

-Rioting never won anything.

So, the square got occupied and rioting continued around the old town for a few nights.

In one of the tents I started to interview people. One girl caught my eye. Short blonde hair and layers of baggy jumpers, and tip-less gloves.

-Can I interview you for folks back in the UK, students?

-You are a journalist?

-Well, a student activist wanna be journalist.

-Sure, let's go somewhere more cosy.

We filtered away from the square, squeezing past drummers and people standing on boxes delivering speeches. The sirens were ringing out all over, and round corners black shapes could be seen running, and smashing and fire-bombing and then squads of cops with shields like Roman legionnaires shuffled down a street as hails of rocks fell down upon them.

We dodged the rioters and hid in alleys from cops and found a pub open. It was a mini brewery, and they made their own beer on the premises.

We sat and a guy came over, she just held up two fingers.

-So, what will happen?

-Difficult to say but I am sceptical, the riots will fade away and it's a question of whether we made enough impact for the occupation of the square to continue and more importantly get more support. People are not rushing to the streets to support us, even though we knew they wouldn't for the centre but now we thought that they would support us against the government. Everyone is always moaning about the corruption, maybe we need something more to ignite the people... say if the government raised the price of beer.

We took our foam heavy mugs and clinked glasses as we looked in each other's eyes, the custom here I had found out.

-Na dravi!

-Cheers, yeah na dravi! Yeah, I wanted to say I haven't seen much evidence of workers on the demos.

-Everyone is more or less happy with their jobs and no one wants to rock the boat too much.

-But I read of some unions on strike for better pay.

-The unions are run by old Stalinists, and yeah, they go on strike but it's all about money, never political and it's always just for their own ends. There's not much solidarity.

-Bit pessimistic if you don't mind me saying.

-Not a pessimist a realist.

-Fair enough.

-Students also have an easy life here, what do they have to fight for? They pay no fees, the live at home for free, there's loads of jobs. It's not the UK.

-You know about our situation.

-Of course.

-So, I have to ask you... was it worth the effort?

-Well, we needed to try.

-Pity really. I was sent here by our Student's Union, who aren't the best let me tell you. We thought this was gonna be something big.

She smiles and sips

-Sorry to disappoint you, but hey we have made contact and it's good to have friends, we may need each other in the future.

The waiter plonked two more beers on the table without being asked.

We smiled at each other and leant back a little to relax. I put my notebook away.

-So, what do you want to do after you finish your studies?

-Not sure, but something in campaigning, or something involving helping people. The homeless, refugees maybe. I went a few times down to Serbia and Hungary, and of course I was involved in the centre here, I am studying political science, so I want to use that in some good way.

-I was in Calais too trying to do what I could to help the refugees, it was a terrible situation.

-I think Hungary and Serbia were worse, but it's not a competition.

We grinned again. I was getting to like her more and more.

-It's frustrating though don't you think?

-I think we can only try and do what we can, it will always be frustrating.

She jumped up from her chair.

-Hey do you want to go to a club? My friend's band is playing there.

–Tonight?

-Yes, why not, the protestors need some entertainment.

We ventured out into the glowing night, the smell of fire was all around, the sirens had quietened a little. The streets seemed less chaotic. We passed the square and apart from folk music on guitars and mellow conversation; all was still.

We went down a basement, down an alley in the old town. Some rock band were blasting out the tunes, just a rock band, nothing special. But the atmosphere was good. We fell into a corner with cushions just off the main area and she introduced me to some of her friends.

We sat next to each other but she talked to everyone, all the time, blurting out this, jabbing her fingers at someone and laughing her head off at other times. People talked to me, everyone was friendly but I wasn't really giving them my full attention, I was mesmerized by Lenka.

She bumped in next to me after she had been to the front and head banged.

Her face was close to mine and she stroked my arm.

-Do you have a girl back home?

-No, not right now.

-Strange answer.

-And you?

-I have no girl but I had a boyfriend till recently.

She giggled

-But I threw him out, he was a slob and too negative, he brought me down... so I booted his arse down the stairs.

She rolled over and laughed loudly.

She got close to me again.

And leant her head on my shoulder, I could feel her breath near my mouth.

-You're not a slob, are you? I know you are positive, but are you a slob?

-I am a famous for my tidiness.

She smiled.

-I thought so, I can always tell, and you smell nice.

-Thanks, err, you too.

-Don't go all shy on me, Englishman.

She leant over and kissed me.

-Let's get out of here. Shall we go back to my apartment?

-I would love to.

-Where's your stuff?

-In a locker in the station.

-OK, we can get a tram from here and then another to my place it's not too far... come, Englishman...

She grabbed me off the floor and out the door.

* * *

Her place was in an old apartment building, high ceilings, metal rails up the four flights of stairs, no lift and lights that you have to keep pressing. Her place was small and cluttered, but cosy. The place was a mess but a stylish mess; French bohemia with a bohemian twist. Throws over everything. Paintings scattered all over, posters tacked up willy-nilly. Books were in piles and the bookshelves stacked with ornaments, pots from her gran probably, and glass vases with fake flowers. Jewellery littered the shelf over the fireplace with a huge mirror mounted from the floor covered in clothes, the rest were thrown on chairs or just the floor.

From the corner kitchenette she got a bottle of Slivovice from a cupboard and two dusty shot glasses. Put them on the old trunk in the middle of the room and then found a record from a pile and placed the needle on some old 60s soul LP. We sank into her couch and drank back a couple of shots. She giggled and on her knees on the couch kissed me passionately. We managed to fumble and roll over to the mattress on the floor and buried ourselves under the goose-feather duvet. Underneath we kissed and laughed and tried to undress each other or sometimes we just flung the things off ourselves. The cat joined us, and I kicked him off before we fucked.

I woke with a sore head and the cat on my back. She was in the corner in a dressing gown making filter coffee.

-Hello, sleepy head. How do you feel?

-Like shit.

-Welcome to Czech, we feel this way many mornings but I can make you better don't worry.

We sat and drank coffee by the open veranda window on two stools and an old Formica kitchen table folded down. She spread out lumps of fat and uncooked bacon on bread and raw onion, radishes and made runny scrambled eggs. The she took the opener on a string and opened two bottles of pivo.

-Typical Czech breakfast. Na Dravi!

-Shit yeah cheers.

After a few more beers and the food I did feel OK actually. We had showers; fucked again; and dressed I kicked the cat one more time as we left the building.

We went to the square to see what was going on, not much. The rioting had stopped and numbers were down. People were sat around talking and messaging.

We went to another beer hall in the evening and I listened to the activists plan new ideas; buildings to squat, centres to be opened, food deliveries and tents to be delivered and theatre for street kids. All good but not the revolution I had come for.

We went back to her flat again, drunk again and fucked again and in the morning, we had pivo again.

After three days I got my shit together to go home, I booked a seat on a train to Berlin and beyond for the afternoon.

We talked about meeting up again, but you know long distance relationships, you could see we both doubted ourselves to carry it through, so made no promises, except that she might visit in the summer and I said I would like to come back, we swapped no addresses; we were already in contact on Facebook and Twitter and WhatsApp.

We went to the station and had a last beer and kissed and smiled at each other.

-Just like a film no?

-Yeah but will you wave a white hanky at me as I look out the window and throw a flower.

-No.

I got the train to Berlin.

About the Author

Nick Gerrard is originally from Birmingham but now living in Olomouc where he writes, proof-reads and edits, (Abridged versions of the classics; like Hemmingway and Orwell) and in between looking after his son Joe, edits and designs Jotters United Lit-zine. Nick has been at one time or another a Chef, activist, union organiser, punk rocker, teacher, traveller and Eco-lodge owner in Malawi and Czech.

More from Nick Gerrard- Collect them all!

- Graffiti Stories by Nick Gerrard

  978-91-986710-1-8
- Punk Novelette by Nick Gerrard

  978-91-986710-8-7

More from Breaking Rules Europe

- Face of Fear by C. Marry Hultman

  978-91-986710-0-1
- Dawson Junior G3 by Brian Wagstaff

  978-91-986710-4-9
- Murder Planet by Adam Carpenter

  978-91-986710-3-2
- New Life Cottage
  978-91-986710-5-6
- Liebe ist Warten

  978-91-986710-7-0
- Musing on Death & Dying

  978-91-986710-6-3
- Earth Door by Cye Thomas

  978-91-986710-2-5

- Lost Lore and Legends – anthology
    - Paperback: 9789198671094
    - Hardcover: 9789198684100

Find us at: www.breakingrulespublishingeuro.com

www.ingramcontent.com/pod-product-compliance
Lightning Source LLC
LaVergne TN
LVHW020030160726
843469LV00044B/1716